From the Files of

Madison Finn

Read all the books about Madison Finn!

Coming Soon!

From the Files of Madison Finn

Save the Date

By Laura Dower

VOLO

HYPERION
New York

Text copyright © 2002 by Laura Dower

From the Files of Madison Finn, Volo, and the Volo colophon are trademarks of Disney Enterprises, Inc.

Printed in the United States of America

First Edition
5 7 9 10 8 6 4

The main body of text of this book is set in 13-point Frutiger Roman.

ISBN 0-7868-1681-3

Visit www.madisonfinn.com

For Dad with love

Chapter 1

Fwwwwackkkkkkkk!

Thunder boomed outside Madison Finn's bedroom window.

"Rowrrrooooooo!" her dog, Phin, barked. He leaped onto the bed, knocking Madison's laptop from its pillow perch.

"Phinnie," Madison cooed, readjusting her computer. "Oh, poor Phinnie. You're not afraid of the storm, are you?"

Shakier than shaky, Phin wormed his pug body near Madison's belly to get warm. She had to maneuver her own body so she could type on her laptop computer *and* snuggle at the same time.

Madison went into her file folders, where she had

been keeping a regular record of life in seventh grade. She thought that files were a great way to keep herself organized. Unfortunately, the opposite seemed to be true today. Her "perfect" system was getting messier and messier. The more things she did in school, after school, and on weekends . . . the more Madison jammed onto new computer file pages. She couldn't keep her facts straight anymore. Just the week before, Madison had forgotten about a Spanish quiz and a math assignment in the same week.

"Rain, rain, go away," Madison chanted. She typed in a brand-new file name.

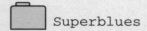 Superblues

Here it is the end of March and I have the seventh-grade superblues. Doesn't that sound like a song?

I can't seem to get ANYTHING done, and I have this MEGA paper due for English honoring women's history that I haven't even started! I haven't done my Spanish homework for a week, and Señora Diaz is going to be so mad. I didn't know life was supposed to be stressed out in seventh grade. Is it just me or what?

Even Mom is superbusy these days with some new movie crew and assignment. Dad is busy, too. Even when we have one of our special dinners, he always has something else on his mind besides me. His girlfriend, Stephanie, says he's working on some new Internet deal. Maybe he's nervous? Ever since Mom and Dad's big D—divorce—last year, things have started getting busier and weirder for all of us.

Rude Awakening: If I figure out how to save time, how can I use it later? That would really help with all this stuff I have to do.

Madison closed her file and popped a brand-new CD-ROM into her laptop. She easily booted up the new software called Calendar Girl that Dad had given her.

With the click of a few keys, Madison found herself at the main menu screen. A stardust trail chased Madison's arrow cursor as it moved across the page. Type flashed blue and pink.

Dear Diary Planner
Go to the Head of the Class
Homework Keeper
Extracurricular Time
Calendar Girl to Do
Friends Contact List

Madison stared at the screen. She didn't know where to mouse-click first.

Drip.

She wiped a wet droplet off her hand. Was Phin drooling again?

Drip. Drip.

It wasn't drool at all.

Looking up over her head, Madison saw another pair of kamikaze drips before they landed. They were coming from the ceiling. The terrible rainstorm had made its way inside Madison's bedroom.

"MOM!" Madison screamed even louder than a thunderclap. Phin jumped and dove off the bed for the closet. "MOM!" she screamed again.

Quickly Madison pulled her laptop to a dry area for safety. She moved her pillows and the afghan, and grabbed her trash basket to put on top of the bed. She hoped that would catch the drips. They were beginning to fall more steadily now, like a leaky faucet.

"Madison?" Mom was breathless from running up the stairs. "You know I hate it when you yell for me like that. What on earth—"

"We have a leak!" Madison screeched, pointing to the wet ceiling. Phin peeked out of the closet.

"Oh, no!" Mom wailed. "You've got to be kidding me!" She dashed out of the room.

"MOM! Where are you going?" Madison yelled. "Mom, get back here. My whole room is going to be underwater if you don't get back here!"

Mom returned a moment later with the phone and the yellow pages. She dialed up a contractor she'd called once before.

"Is this Dickson Fix-It?" Mom asked. "This is

Francine Finn over on Blueberry Street. We seem to have this leak upstairs. . . ."

Madison sat down near her desk and watched, helpless, as the drips kept dripping into her orange plastic wastepaper basket. Madison wanted to say, "Mom, why don't you call *Dad* instead?" but that wouldn't have been a proper suggestion. Not since the big D.

Dad *never* freaked out during emergencies like Mom did. During the winter, the boiler had stopped working, and Mom had almost exploded the house trying to fix it alone. Had Dad been around, it would have been repaired without a second thought. He would have had this roof leak solved in a flash.

Fwwwwackkkkkkkk!

A new bolt of thunder cracked. The rain started to fall harder again. So did the drips. Phin scooted into the closet again.

"What is going to happen to my room?" Madison cried. "My stuff is all going to be ruined. MOM! Aimee's coming over soon!"

Even though it was Sunday and a school night, Madison's best friend, Aimee Gillespie, was coming over to eat dinner and do homework. Aimee's parents had to go somewhere for a business dinner with some other booksellers. Her father's store, The Book Web, had won some kind of local business award.

Madison's other best friend, Fiona Waters, had been invited to come over for the study session, too, but she had a family dinner to attend. So it was two neighborhood BFFs instead of three.

"Now, just calm down, Maddie," Mom said. "You can bring your laptop downstairs when Aimee comes. We'll move you into the den until this gets fixed."

Dingdong.

"Aimee's here NOW!" Madison squealed. "She's going to absolutely freak out when she sees this!"

Madison skipped downstairs to answer the front door as a very wet Aimee pushed her way inside.

"Oh my God! My mom had to *drive* me over here. It is soooo wet out!" Aimee cried.

Phinnie squirmed around on the wet floor by Aimee's feet, his tail squiggling. Even with all the rain, Phin could smell Aimee's dog, Blossom, all over her jeans. He sniffed and sniffed. Aimee just giggled and kept shaking her wet head. She looked like she was doing some kind of rain dance. As a ballerina, Aimee did *everything* with dancing flair.

"Here, use this, Aim," Madison said, handing Aimee a towel from the downstairs bathroom.

"Thanks!" Aimee said, still twirling. "So what's up?"

"My whole room is LEAKING!" Madison launched into a full explanation of the disaster in her bedroom.

"Whoa," Aimee said. "That sounds pretty bad." She reached into her bag and pulled out a bottle of blue nail polish. The jar said, ARE YOU BLUE?

"What's that for?" Madison asked.

"I got it at the store today. I could paint your nails tonight," Aimee said with a wide grin. "This color will look so perfect on you."

"Really?" Madison asked.

"I think we should blow off homework and have a beauty night," Aimee said. "At least before we eat dinner."

"I have an English paper to write," Madison said.

"Yeah, but this will be more fun," Aimee argued.

"I guess you're right," Madison said with a giant smile. "I wanted to show you this new lip gloss I just bought, too. Let me get it."

Madison reached over for her orange bag, sitting on a table in the hall, and fished around inside. First she pulled out a few books, a green notebook, a pencil case, a pair of socks. . . .

"What is all *that*?" Aimee said, laughing.

"Oh, just stuff I really need," Madison replied. She took out a calculator, a package of gum, a purple bandanna. . . .

"Wait. I've never seen that scarf. When did you get that?" Aimee asked.

"Last month at the mall. I forgot I left it in here."

Madison still couldn't find the lip gloss, so she turned her bag upside down and dumped everything else right onto the hall carpet. There on the carpet were two neon-colored rubber bands, two chewed-on pen caps, a pen that had just started leaking (luckily into an old tissue), a rabbit's foot key chain, and one large piece of light-blue crumpled paper that appeared to be stuck to some chewing gum.

"Bummer!" Madison said. "I must have left it in my locker."

She was about to shove all of the objects right back into the bag when she noticed the crumpled paper. She unfolded the sheet quickly.

SAVE THE DATE.

Madison read the paper aloud. It was a permission slip for the science field trip that she was supposed to have returned to her science teacher a week earlier.

"Oh my God, Maddie! You never handed that in?" Aimee said when she saw the sheet.

Madison bit her lip. "Is that a bad thing?"

"Well, it's after the deadline," Aimee said.

"Yeah, b-but . . ." Madison stammered. "What do you mean, I can't go?"

"Usually they're pretty strict about deadlines," Aimee said.

"I am such a space case," Madison said, frowning.

"Maddie, I'm sure you'll be able to go. Just get your mom to sign the slip right now. She can explain to the teacher what happened," Aimee said.

"MOM!" Without missing a beat, Madison yelled for her mother. "MOM!" She was determined to get her permission slip signed right now.

Mom flung open her office door with a huff. "Madison Francesca Finn, haven't I asked you a zillion times to please—"

"Mom, will you sign this?" Madison shoved the rumpled, gum-stained blue slip and a ballpoint pen under Mom's nose.

"What is it?" Mom asked, grabbing the slip to read it. "'Save the Date'? Where did this come from?"

"Her book bag," Aimee chimed in.

Madison gave Aimee's left shoulder a thwack.

"I meant to give it to you before, Mom, but it got stuck—"

"I can see that," Mom said, fingers on the dried-up gum. She signed on the dotted line. "This trip is in a couple of days. Are you prepared? It says you have to do some research in advance."

"Oh, no!" Aimee chimed in again. "That's just stuff we do during regular class. She's totally prepared for the trip. . . ."

Madison smiled. Aimee had come to her rescue, and that got Mom to stop asking questions. Mom handed the signed slip back to Madison.

"Next time you get one of these, give it to me right away," Mom said.

Dingdong.

Mom threw her hands into the air. "*Now* what?" She raced over to the door and opened it with a flourish.

"Oh!" Mom exclaimed. "It's you!"

The Dickson Fix-It guy had finally arrived, with his gray hair and clothes drenched from the rain. His shirt read WILLIAM on the pocket in red embroidered letters. When he smiled, Madison saw a huge gap between his front teeth.

"Name's Billy," he said gruffly, shaking Mom's hand. "You must be . . ."

"Fran Finn," Mom said with a smile.

Fwwwwwackkkkkkkk!

Lightning and thunder flared up again, and Aimee and Madison screamed, grabbing each other around the waist. The hall lights flickered.

"Welcome to the fun house," Mom said to Billy with an exasperated sigh. She led him inside. As he walked into the hallway, Madison noticed Mom was still smiling.

And Billy was smiling back.

"He's kind of cute," Aimee whispered, elbowing Madison in the side. "Don't you think?"

Madison made a face. "Eeeeeeew," she said softly. "He's old."

"Let's go get that leak!" Billy said. "Where do I need to go?"

Mom laughed even though he hadn't said anything funny. As they walked over to the staircase, Billy stepped carefully over the pile of stuff Madison had emptied out of her bag in the hallway.

"What is *this*?" Mom said, pointing to the pile.

"Oh. Nothing. I'll pick it up later, Mom." Madison groaned. "I promise."

Madison expected an instant lecture. Lucky for her, Mom didn't make a scene or say another word. She just turned and smiled at Billy again.

"The problem is coming from my daughter's bedroom," Mom said as she led him upstairs. Billy hovered behind her like an insect, his tools dangling and clanging on his belt.

"Come on, Aimee," Madison grumbled. She grabbed Aimee's wrist and headed upstairs. "I want to keep an eye on things."

Chapter 2

Aimee gasped when they walked into Madison's bedroom. It was wetter than wet—and the wastebasket wasn't doing much good anymore. New leaks had started in different spots on the ceiling.

"It's all coming from the same main leak," Billy said, reaching up to touch the ceiling. "It's traveling along the beams in the ceiling. You got a chimney on this side of the house? Had any problems with that roof?"

Mom shrugged. "I don't have a clue," she said. "I thought we were fine. We never had a leak before."

Billy opened the window and stuck his head out into the rain. He said if he arched his back, he could see the chimney. Mom went over to the window to make sure he wouldn't fall out.

"Please be careful," she said, flailing her arms.

She bobbed and weaved herself to avoid getting pelted by raindrops. "Isn't that dangerous?"

Aimee thought Billy was cool.

Madison thought he was acting like a show-off.

"You got a bigger problem than one little leak," Billy said, climbing back inside.

"How much?" Mom asked. She sat on the windowsill and groaned.

Billy smiled, and his teeth gleamed. "Well, I think your chimney is busted and some of the shingles out there need to be replaced. You have some rotten wood and corrosion. And unfortunately, with this rain, I can't really do much until it dries up. . . ."

"Oh!" Mom sighed. But then she smiled. "But it *can* be fixed? You can fix it?"

"That's why we call the company Dickson Fix-It, ma'am."

"Please. Call *me* Frannie," Mom said.

Madison crossed her arms against her chest and made a face. How could Mom be acting so nice to this total stranger when there was a total disaster in her bedroom? And why was she still smiling?

Aimee was getting a little restless, too. "Let's go back downstairs, Maddie," Aimee pleaded. "I have something to show you—and we have to paint our nails, remember?"

"Yeah, yeah," Madison said. She didn't want to leave all her stuff. She didn't want to leave Mom, either.

Before they went back down, Mom asked the girls to help move some of Madison's things out of the way and against the walls. They pushed the purple inflatable chair over by the closet, covered the bed in plastic, and made sure no clothing, stuffed animals, or posters were in a potential "wet zone." Then Madison followed her BFF back downstairs, reluctantly.

Sharp rain plinked against the windows in the den. There was a flash of yellow in the evening sky that made the room glow. Madison counted one, two, three until a thunderbolt cracked. The storm sounded like it was churning around the house and trees in the backyard.

"I have to show you my new pictures!" Aimee said, rushing over to her schoolbag. She pulled out a fat blue portfolio. "I need you to help me pick one out for the ballet revue program."

Aimee pulled Madison over to the couch and sat her down.

"Do you like the one with my hair in the bun or a French twist?" Aimee asked as she took out more photos. "What do you think of this one?" Aimee held up a photograph of her in a pink-and-blue pastel leotard. "I look way too fat, right?"

"Huh?" Madison sighed. She got up and wandered over by the stairway to see if she could hear anything else from upstairs.

"Maddie?" Aimee asked. She held up another

14

photo that looked *exactly* like the first one. "What about this?"

"You always look great," Madison said, distracted. She could still hear faint noises from upstairs. *Laughter. A hammer. More laughter.*

Aimee held the two pictures up again for a side-by-side comparison. "I think I like this one better. Don't you?"

Madison was staring up the stairway, trying to hear the conversation between her mom and Billy.

"Earth to Madison! I just asked you a question," Aimee said.

"Sorry," Madison said. She took the photographs from Aimee and picked one. "I like this. You look pretty in this one."

Mom came down the stairs. "Well! We're in capable hands with Billy. Isn't he great?"

"Great," Madison said, not feeling the situation was great in any way.

"Anyone hungry for some dinner?" Mom asked the pair.

Madison and Aimee followed her into the kitchen. Since pizza was the ultimate friend food, Mom ordered a large one with mushrooms and pepperoni.

"I think that Billy guy is so weird," Madison said to her mom.

"Oh, Maddie! But he's so nice." Mom laughed. "Billy works as a cameraman for a film company.

15

Isn't it a small world that we both work in the industry? He does contracting work on the side when he's not filming. Actually, Billy and I have a lot in common. Isn't that funny?"

"Hysterical," Madison said. She wanted Mom to stop smiling and *stop* saying his name. The word *Billy* was really bothering Madison, like a pesky mosquito buzzing at her ears.

"Can I show you my ballet pictures, Mrs. Finn?" Aimee asked, pushing her overflowing portfolio onto the countertop.

"Of course," Mom said, clearing a space on the kitchen table. "Let's see what you've got."

Madison leaned in close to Aimee. Looking at the ballet photos again was the last thing she felt like doing, but it was *way* better than talking about the things Mom had on her mind.

Like Billy the bug.

Even with the rainstorm, the pizza-delivery guy made it to Madison's house in under a half hour—a time frame that's 100 percent guaranteed or else the pizza was free. Madison, Aimee, and Mom ate it with salad that Mom threw together. They had store-bought brownies for dessert, but Aimee only ate a corner of one.

By the time they'd eaten pizza, Billy had surveyed the upstairs room completely and given Mom a rough estimate of the work that would need to be done. He said that he'd come back to check on the roof and attic the next day. Mom chatted with him like he was some kind of old pal. Madison squirmed every time he grinned his gap-toothed grin.

After Billy left, Mom headed into her office to do some film-editing work while Madison and Aimee disappeared to do their homework. At least they intended to do their assignments. Instead of math books, however, they pulled out Aimee's manicure stuff. Aimee painted Madison's nails a perfect blue to match Madison's rainy-day mood.

"Let's go online and find Fiona," Aimee suggested when she'd finished nail painting.

"But she's at that family dinner," Madison said. "And I can't type or anything with my nails like this." She blew on them to make them dry faster.

"Fiona's dinner must be over by now," Aimee said, looking at her watch. "And I can type for you so your nails don't get messed up."

They set up the laptop on the desk in the den and logged on to bigfishbowl.com. Aimee typed while Madison leaned over Aimee's shoulder for assistance.

"You have to give your password," Aimee said when she saw the password prompt. Madison grabbed a pencil to punch her supersecret password on the keyboard without messing up her nails.

```
Screen Name: MADFINN
Supersecret Password: ********
```

The waiting room inside bigfishbowl.com was packed with members. Aimee scrolled down the list of special rooms.

```
Soccer rules!!!!!!!!
(11 fish)
```

"I bet she's in there," Aimee said right away. "She's such a soccer maniac."

But Madison told Aimee to keep looking. She knew Fiona would wait somewhere else where they'd *all* be more likely to hang out.

```
******animal lovers here*****
(23 fish)
Keypal Kingdom
(8 fish)
Junior High—enter at ur own risk!
(41 fish)
```

"There!" Madison blurted. "I bet she's in that junior-high room. We went in there once when she was over."

Aimee glanced at the list of forty-one kids' screen names.

```
Crazy_boyz
Luv4ever
```

```
HelPer
Peacefish
Willyd00
Luckyduck
987goforit
lovetoPARTY
barbeedoll
Flowr99
BryanSarah
Wetwinz
```

"Wetwinz!" Aimee said. Fiona was online with the screen name both Aimee and Madison knew. Fiona had selected the name to match that of her twin brother, Chet. His was *Wetwins* with an *s*. It stood for "We are twins!"

"Wait a second," Madison said, pointing to the name *Flowr99*. "Look who's in the chat room with her—Poison Ivy Daly!"

Aimee didn't recognize Ivy Daly's screen name. "Is Flowr99 Ivy's screen name? She's a *poisonous* flower if she's any kind of flower!"

Madison checked her buddy list. Her keypal Bigwheels was also online. Madison and Bigwheels had first met online inside a bigfishbowl.com chat room called GO FISHY. After a few chats, Madison learned that Bigwheels was greater than great at dishing out advice—especially when it came to friendship.

But she couldn't talk to her right now. She'd have to give her a shout-out later, after Aimee went home.

Suddenly, Fiona's screen name appeared on the buddy list. "Look who's here!" Aimee said excitedly. She typed a quick Insta-Message and hit SEND.

```
<MadFinn>: HELLOOOOOO FIONA!
<Wetwinz>: Hi Maddie
<MadFinn>: and Aimee too how wuz
    dinner???
<Wetwinz>: Boring. I wish I was
    there w/u guys
<MadFinn>: did u get caught in the
    rain tonight
<Wetwinz>: no but lightning hit a
    tree on my block!
<MadFinn>: =8-o
<Wetwinz>: it fell on Ridge Rd.
<MadFinn>: WOW did Egg call u?
```

Madison gave Aimee a light punch on the shoulder. "Aimee!" she said. "You aren't supposed to ask her about that."

Egg was the nickname of their best guy friend, Walter Diaz. Fiona liked him—a lot.

```
<Wetwinz>: Yeah Egg called tonite
<MadFinn>: HE DID??? WHAT DID HE
    SAY?
```

```
<Wetwinz>: he wanted homework pages.
   That's all
<MadFinn>: YR he just wanted reason
   to call u
```

Madison wanted to erase what Aimee wrote. She knew Fiona could be a little sensitive about the whole Egg thing. She leaned over Aimee and tried to punch in a message of her own.

```
<MadFinn>: dont lis ten to Am ee!
```

"Maddie, stop that!" Aimee yelped. "You'll mess up your nails!"

```
<Wetwinz>: LOL which 1 of u is
   writing 2 me?
<MadFinn>: Maddi so wha else s gon
   on?
```

Madison could barely type in the awkward position she was in. And her nails were getting a little smudged.

"Oh, Maddie, will you just let me type, please?" Aimee said, giggling. "I won't ask about Egg anymore, okay? I promise. Cross my heart."

Madison leaned back again. "Okay. But you promised."

```
<MadFinn>: Aimee typing now—so what
   else is new
```

```
<Wetwinz>: well I ordered my GLASSES
   today
<MadFinn>: Ooooooh how do they look?
   Didja get the wire ones or the
   ones that look like turtle
   shells?
<Wetwinz>: tortoise AND my mom got
   me a special strap so I can wear
   them when I play soccer 2
<MadFinn>: I bet u look groageous
<MadFinn>: I mean GORGEOUS
<Wetwinz>: LOL I wish I was there
   w/you guys
<MadFinn>: come oVER! It's only a
   short walk.
<Wetwinz>: it's raining hard
<MadFinn>: ok then c u 18r
<Wetwinz>: LYLAS
```

"Girls!" Mom called out. "GIRLS!"

Mom interrupted their online conversation with the dangle of car keys. She was ready to take Aimee home.

"Already?" Aimee protested.

"It's nine o'clock and it's a school night," Mom said.

While Aimee and Mom went to get into the car, Madison dragged Phin outside to say good-bye and get in a quick walk at the same time. Sidewalks were off-limits for pugs during lightning storms, so

Phinnie stayed very close to home. He nosed happily around the front steps only.

"See you in school tomorrow, Maddie," Aimee yelled as the car pulled out of the driveway. "Bye!"

"Thanks for my nails!" Madison yelled back. She waved good-bye to Aimee from the front porch. "I loooove the color!"

"Rowrrrooooof!" Phinnie barked his own good-bye, shook the rain off his fur, and headed for the front door.

Madison unhooked his leash and went back into the den.

In the half-darkened room, she saw that her laptop screen was lit. She and Aimee had forgotten to log off the bigfishbowl.com site. To Madison's surprise, there was a new e-mail waiting in her e-mailbox.

From: Bigwheels
To: MadFinn
Subject: School Trips
Date: Sun 25 Mar 7:36 PM
What's up? I went shopping w/my mother and my cousin today and bought this GREAT shirt. It will look amazing this wk when we go on our school mountain trip. Everything about the trip is planned: we're saving the whole date for hiking

and writing. Sometimes my school
plans cool trips. We even have
classes outside once in a while!
Plus we get to pick our own
partners and of course I am pairing
up w/my BFF Lainie.

Have u been on any major school
trips this yr?

Yours till the peanut butters,

Bigwheels

P.S. I had a peanut butter for a
sandwich today—my new fave food.
What is ur fave food?

Madison couldn't believe that she and her keypal
were both going on school trips in the same week—
or that Bigwheels liked peanut butter as much as
Madison did. They had so much in common.

She looked down at her polished fingernails and
smiled.

The nails were still blue, of course. But thanks to
her friends, online and off, Madison wasn't feeling
blue anymore.

She could hardly wait for the week to begin.

Chapter 3

Madison had to stop by her locker to grab all of her science books before Monday's classes started. She wanted to be extra prepared. That way, Mr. Danehy would be impressed and would be more likely to accept her very late permission slip for the field trip.

As she was standing in front of her locker, Hart Jones and Chet Waters passed by on their way to science class.

"Hey, Finnster!" Hart yelled.

"Yeah, how's it going, Finnster!" Chet said, making fun of Hart's nickname for Madison.

They rushed up behind Madison, but she just made a face at them and looked in the other direction. Finnster was a name her secret crush, Hart Jones, used. But now that Fiona's twin brother, Chet, started calling her that name, it sounded a little different.

Madison tried opening her locker, but she couldn't remember the combination.

She watched as Hart and Chet walked away down the hall.

What was her code?

Madison pulled on the lock and tried another set of numbers. But that didn't open it, either.

Brrrrrriing.

The first set of bells rang. She had to dash. The books would have to wait. Madison took off for Mr. Danehy's room, still trying to remember the numbers that would open her locker. Why was she forgetting everything these days?

Luckily there were quite a few kids who hadn't yet made it into the classroom, so Madison entered the room without anyone noticing. Mr. Danehy wasn't even there yet. Madison sat down at her assigned seat right next to her lab partner, Poison Ivy.

"Nice nails," Ivy mumbled. She sounded like she had a little cold.

Madison held out one hand to admire them. "Yeah, it's a cool color."

Ivy held up her own hand. She had the exact same color on her nails; only her nails were longer and more manicured than Madison's.

"Ahhh . . . ahhhh . . ." Ivy started to sniffle, and Madison handed her a tissue from her book bag.

"Choooooo!" Ivy exploded in a giant sneeze.

"Nice job, Ivy!" Chet yelled from across the room. "We felt that one all the way over here."

Ivy wiped her nose and shook her head. "Dork."

"I know you are, but what am I?" Chet shot back.

Ivy just rolled her eyes and looked over at Madison. "Can I have another tissue? Thanks."

Chet practiced being annoying, Madison was sure of that. She knew what a pest he was because Fiona was always complaining about him. But in science class he was the absolute *worst*. Chet's favorite *annoying* thing to do was imitate their teacher, Mr. Danehy. He put on Mr. Danehy's strange accent that no one understood but everyone joked about.

"Today weeee will beeee studying the life cycle of zeeee beee!" Chet announced, standing in front of Mr. Danehy's desk.

Everyone burst into laughter.

"Do us all a favor and sit down," Ivy yelled.

Madison grinned. For the first time in a long time, she was totally on Ivy's side.

"Yeah, Chet. Quit acting like a moron," one of Ivy's drones, Rose Snyder, said from a row behind them.

"Excuse me?" Chet said, laughing himself. "I'm not the one who just sprayed snot all over the room."

Ivy stood up. "Why don't you just stop?" she said. "Quit acting like a jerk."

Chet scoffed at both of them. "Girls are the jerks."

"Yeah!" another boy yelled.

Even Hart started laughing, which Madison couldn't believe. Most of the girls in the room booed. It was chaos as girls left their desks to gather on one side of the room and boys gathered on the other side. A kind of war had been declared when everyone least expected it. Everyone was *yelling*.

"What is all this ruckus about?" Mr. Danehy said as he strolled into the classroom later than usual. He slammed his briefcase onto his desk and clapped wildly. "What is going on?"

Chet dashed over to his chair. Everyone else hushed up. They all sat down close to where they'd been standing.

"I SAID . . . what is all this ruckus about? Does someone want to help me out here? Ms. Snyder? You were one of the girls booing. What is going on? Do you think that you can just do whatever you like when I am not in the room?"

Rose shrank into her new chair. "No, Mr. Danehy," she said.

Ivy raised her hand from the back of the room. "We were just—"

"ENOUGH!" Mr. Danehy yelled. He yanked a stack of papers out of his briefcase and handed it to two kids in the front row. "Take one and pass it along."

Madison glanced around. She didn't know what to do. Her plan to gently pass the late permission slip to Mr. Danehy had been foiled by this spontaneous classroom war.

Ivy passed Madison her copy of the trip instructions sheet. Written in bold across the top was a simple heading.

SCIENCE TRIP TO FAR HILLS NATURE TRAILS:
Wednesday, March 28

Madison read down the sheet for information. Luckily she'd read most of the textbook chapters on earth science and animals that covered what they'd be seeing at the nature center. Unluckily the list of things they had to see and record was way longer than she'd expected. This field trip was going to be hard work.

Places to Visit:
1. Field habitat
2. Forest habitat
3. Duck pond
4. Butterfly zone
5. Apiary

"Now, I want you to read this very carefully, students," Mr. Danehy explained. "What I have organized here is a little friendly competition. When we go to the nature center, I would like two teams to gather as much information as possible about the animals and natural life in all of the places I've listed here. You will find more specific questions at the bottom of your sheet."

Madison flipped the paper over. He had questions and then questions about those questions. This would take *forever* to complete.

Mr. Danehy continued. "The two teams will bring their results back to class for an oral presentation and debate in class. Is that clear?"

Chet had to speak. "What teams are you talking about, Mr. Danehy?" he asked. "We don't have teams."

Mr. Danehy paused and leaned forward against his desk. "Quite right," he said, thinking. "No teams *yet*." He raised his arms. "What's easiest? How about this side of the room will compete against this side of the room? How's that?"

The kids glanced around at one another.
Didn't he notice that one side was only girls?
And the other side was only boys?

"Mr. Danehy," a girl from the front said softly. "Do you think that's a fair way to split up the room?"

"Yeah!" Chet yelled.

"What are you talking about? It couldn't be more equal. There are exactly the same numbers of seats on each side." He counted them out loud. "Numbers here are very fair. And scientific."

Everyone sighed. Sometimes Mr. Danehy noticed little details and forgot to notice big ones. And once he made up his mind, there was no changing it. He thought he was being fair.

But without realizing it, he'd just drawn battle lines for a battle of the sexes.

"Well, that sounds like discrimination," Madison's school friend Lindsay Frost said in the lunchroom. Madison explained the story of science to everyone seated at the orange table in the cafeteria.

"Discrimination? What is that, exactly?" Aimee asked.

"Picking one group over another," Lindsay explained. "But *unfairly*."

Fiona piped up. She shared a far-out story about an elementary school teacher she had in California. He got into trouble because the school said he picked on girls more than boys during class. Parents thought he played favorites.

"All teachers have favorites," Madison said. "I know mine do."

"You are so right," Lindsay said.

"I don't mind it when it's me, of course . . ." Aimee added, chuckling under her breath.

The whole table laughed.

"But Mr. Danehy is different. He isn't discriminating or whatever you call it. He doesn't think that way," Madison explained. "I still don't think he even noticed that one side was girls and the other was boys. He just counted heads. He's scientific about *everything*."

"Still," Aimee said, drinking from a juice box, "the whole setup is just freaky. It's like the Dark Ages or something. How could Mr. Danehy not notice?"

"I think it's funny," Madison said. "The boys in our class *are* total geeks. And now we have the chance to make Chet eat his words. No offense, Fiona. I know he's your twin brother and all, but he is such . . ."

"A PAIN!" Fiona laughed. "I'd like a chance to show up my brother, too."

During the course of their lunchroom conversation, Madison discovered some other surprising news. Mr. Danehy's science class wasn't only the one group in the entire seventh grade that matched boys versus girls. They were also the only class to have a mile-long list of things to explore, the only class that had a list of questions to answer, and the only class that had to do a presentation after the trip was over.

"The whole thing is just wicked unfair," Fiona said. She pushed her lunch tray away. "You have to win that challenge, Maddie."

Ivy Daly strolled by, followed by her drones, Rose and Joanie.

"Hey, Madison," Ivy called out.

Madison smiled. "Hey," she said.

"See you around," Ivy said, and walked past the group.

"What was *that*?" Aimee said, faking shock. "Did you just make nice with the enemy?"

"No," Madison said. "She only said hello because we're science partners. Enemy status will return to normal after the science project is over. You watch. If it's boys versus girls, I have to make a truce with Ivy. We're both girls, so we're on the same side."

"No, *you're* a girl and she's . . ." Lindsay's voice trailed off. "She's a weirdo."

Fiona giggled.

"Maddie, you didn't even tell me if Mr. Danehy accepted your permission slip today," Aimee said.

"Yes," Madison said. "Of course he was a big grouch after what happened, but he said I could go. He didn't even notice that it had dried gum on it."

Aimee let out a giant "HA!"

"Hey, how are we all supposed to go on the same trip and have fun when we all have different assignments?" Fiona asked. She had a spaced-out look on her face.

Lindsay agreed. "Does that mean we can't go around together or be bus partners?"

"Oh my God, I didn't think of that!" Aimee said. "We have to be bus buddies."

Fiona laughed. "You sound like you're in third grade, Aim!"

Madison laughed, too. "Will you be my bus buddy, Aimee?" she teased.

Aimee stood up with her lunch tray. "You guys

are cruel," she said. "I'm SERIOUS! You ARE!"

Within moments, the four friends were laughing and talking at the same time. They would do whatever they could to beat the boys, and be bus buddies.

On the way out of the cafeteria, Madison, Aimee, Fiona, and Lindsay almost plowed into Egg and his pal Drew.

"Hey, you guys," Drew said.

Egg grunted in their direction, too. "Hey, guys."

The four girls looked at each other.

Lindsay cracked a smile. "We're not guys," she said.

"We're *girls*," Aimee blurted, and took off down the hall.

"What's that supposed to mean?" Egg yelled.

Fiona smiled coyly. "Sorry, Egg," she said, starting to explain.

Madison grabbed her arm to stop her from saying anything more. "Look, we gotta fly," Madison said, tugging Fiona away from the boys.

Fiona smiled again. Egg was scratching his head with bewilderment.

"They're just wacko," Egg said to Drew.

Drew shrugged. "I guess."

"Later for them," Egg added.

Drew nodded.

But when Madison glanced around, she saw Egg watching Fiona all the way down the hall.

Chapter 4

After school, Madison headed upstairs to the library media center to do research for an English paper for Women's History Month. Her English class had devoted the entire month of March to women writers and suffragettes. Some boys in class complained about this, asking why there was no such thing as "Men's History Month." Mr. Gibbons didn't really have an answer for that except to remind everyone when papers were due.

So far Madison had narrowed down her essay choices to Amelia Earhart, Eleanor Roosevelt, and Madonna.

She went online to look for information. Mr. Gibbons had posted a "teacher page" on the school Web site with specifics about what needed to be in the essay. That was where Madison looked first.

There were new, bold graphics on the school's

home page—a long way from when the page was launched. Students loved helping Mrs. Wing with the development of the site. One of Madison's friends, Drew Maxwell, had recently downloaded new photos of the school building, faculty, and students.

```
       WELCOME TO FAR HILLS JUNIOR HIGH
              1753 Far Hills Avenue
               Far Hills, New York
        School Principal: Mr. Joe Bernard
     Assistant Principal: Ms. Bonnie Goode

          Web page designed and created
            by FH faculty and students
```

Madison scanned the list of pages on the site. It was so much longer now! More than half the teachers posted homework and projects for students to access. The lists were divided by classes. Eighth and ninth grade had their own sets of pages.

```
                CLASS SEVEN TEAM
     Coordinators: Suresh Dhir, Madison Finn,
                  Dana Newman
     Data entry: Ramon Madrigal, Drew Maxwell,
                  Loren Young
     Online programs: Walter Diaz, Midori Lo
        Student advisor: Mrs. Isabel Wing
```

<u>Seventh Grade MENU</u>
Schedules
Teacher Assignments
Clubs & Organizations
Sports & Teams
Field Trips (Coming Soon!)
The Far Hills Journal (7)
School Events
Contact Information & Other Links

Madison found Mr. Gibbons's page, but he didn't have much there to help her write her paper. Then she went to the Bigfishbowl search engine and plugged in the name *Amelia Earhart.* She found the best resource right away—a Web site devoted entirely to her subject.

<u>The Amelia Earhart Web Site</u>
Biography | Quotes | Photos | Achievements
| Links
Description: Learn about the famous woman
who wanted to fly
Category: Society> History> United States>
People> Earhart
More results—Similar pages—Index.org

After reading a few documents and looking at photographs on Amelia's Web site, Madison returned to her search engine to plug in the name *Madonna* next. Up on the screen it said 362,411 sites had been found. Madison gulped. She didn't have time to look through even half of those pages. Most of them were fan sites, anyway.

She plugged in *Eleanor Roosevelt* to see where that led her. *Success!* By searching only a few pages on a few different sites, Madison learned all she needed to write a good paper. She learned that Eleanor Roosevelt had been the First Lady of our country and an activist for human rights. Plus she had actually been an honorary chairman of a foundation for . . . Amelia Earhart! Roosevelt helped to organize a group that granted money to young girls who wanted to study science and sociology. Madison scribbled down the word *sociology* because she wasn't sure exactly what it meant.

It's like everyone is somehow connected, Madison thought. Even famous people from history.

"Hey, study head!" Someone crept up behind Madison. "Surprise!"

"I thought you had soccer practice," Madison said.

Fiona chuckled. "I did, silly. Like an hour ago. It's after four o'clock."

Madison looked up at the wall clock in the library and gasped. "How did it get to be so late?" she said. She'd lost complete track of the time.

The month before, the media center had

acquired three new library computers for student use. This meant that sign-ups for computers weren't as restricted as before. It also meant that it was way easier to lose track of time.

Madison saved the search information on Amelia, Eleanor, and Madonna onto a disk.

"Are you getting ready for that science assignment?" Fiona asked.

Madison shook her head. "English paper."

"Why do you have so much more homework than me?" Fiona said.

"Lucky, I guess." Madison moaned, packing up her orange bag. "I always have too much to do."

As they walked across the library, Fiona turned around and looked back into a reading room. She glanced over at the other computer terminals, too, looking for someone.

Madison knew who she was looking for.

Egg.

On the way out, the girls passed by Lindsay, who was curled up in a chair, reading a book about field habitats.

"Maddie!" Lindsay whispered loudly.

Madison turned around. "Hey, Lindsay," she said.

Fiona smiled. "Look, I have to run down to my gym locker for a sec. Forgot my sweater. I'll meet you out front, okay?"

As Fiona dashed off, Hart Jones appeared. He appeared from nowhere.

Lindsay kept tossing her hair to one side even though it wasn't that long. Madison could tell that Lindsay thought Hart was cute, too. Madison, on the other hand, couldn't get the morning's science class out of her mind. All she saw when she looked at Hart was him laughing in a sea of annoying boys in the middle of Mr. Danehy's class.

"Hey, Finnster, what are you doing here?" Hart asked. He was trying to be nice, but the nicer he tried to be, the more Madison's skin itched.

It itched like she wanted to be anywhere but here.

"So you're getting ready for science, huh?" Hart asked.

"We both are," Lindsay spoke up. "We have so much to do before that field trip, you know? And I haven't even—"

"Doesn't anyone else have other homework besides me?" Madison asked. "I have science, English, and social studies reading. An essay. A math pop quiz coming up . . ."

Hart laughed. Madison wanted to sock him.

"Yeah, I have other work, too." He groaned. "Oh, well. I guess I'll get it done sometime."

Abruptly Madison turned on her heel. "I have to go, Lindsay. See you later, all right?"

Lindsay blinked. "Sure. Yeah. Okay."

Hart started to say, "Hey, Finnster, where are you—?" But before he could finish, Madison was out the door and down the stairs.

Fiona was waiting by the front lobby, and they walked home together.

Mom wasn't home when Madison arrived. Phin came scrambling to the front door with his tail wagging like a windup toy. He had to go out—*fast*.

Today was a lazy dog-walking day. It had to be. Madison had to do her homework, clean up her wet room, and check on her keypal Bigwheels. Even more important, she had to push thoughts of Hart Jones out of her head *completely*. She walked Phin into the backyard and around the house.

"Hey, down there!" a voice called from the roof.

Madison looked up to see Billy the contractor, perched up on a ladder by the chimney.

She waved. "Uh . . . hello."

"Your mom said you'd be home soon. She just ran to the store. We've found the leak up here!" he said cheerily, waving his hammer. "Your room will be back to normal soon."

Madison shrugged. "Okay. Whatever."

Phin was rolling around in the grass, scratching his back. Madison pulled on his leash. She wanted to go back inside. She needed to check on her stuff.

"See you around!" Billy called out. He started hammering again.

When she got back inside the house, Madison immediately grabbed her book bag from the kitchen and climbed the stairs to her room. Although the window was open and Billy had been inside the room, he hadn't fixed anything inside yet. Madison's entire bedroom still smelled like wet, woolly sheep. She wondered if the smell would ever come out.

Since her room and printer were still "under the weather" (literally), Madison decided to print out her Women's History Month project research disk on Mom's printer downstairs. So she went into Mom's office to hook it up.

After she booted up Mom's computer, Madison decided she'd check her e-mail before doing any homework.

She had oodles of messages.

FROM	SUBJECT
✉ TheEggMan	New scrn name
✉ Dantheman Re:	New scrn name
✉ 1234Gotcha	XXX RATED
✉ Boop-Dee-Doop	Crazy Clearance
✉ JeffFinn	Love you

Egg was first. He had sent e-mail because he had changed his screen name and he wanted everyone to know. Dan Ginsburg, another friend of Madison's from school and the animal shelter, wrote back a funny response. He copied everyone on his reply.

From: Dantheman
To: TheEggMan

Cc: MadFinn, BalletGrl, W_Wonka7,
Wetwinz, Wetwins, Sk8ingboy,
Dantheman, Artsy00
Subject: Re: New scrn name
Date: Mon 26 Mar 3:11 PM
Yo! whassup with our scrn names now
they are like the same! Why don't u
call yourself EggDrop or maybe
Egghead instead LOL. Call me l8r
g8r.

From: TheEggMan
To: MadFinn, BalletGrl, W_Wonka7,
Wetwinz, Wetwins, Sk8ingboy,
Dantheman, Artsy00
Subject: New scrn name
Date: Mon 26 Mar 3:01 PM
my old name Eggaway stinx so frm
now on change ur mailbx to
TheEggMan. C u bye

Boys could act so dorky sometimes, Madison
thought as she read their messages. Online, in
school, and no matter where else she went,
Madison's friends who were boys had been acting
like Weirdos (with a capital *W*) lately.

Maybe Mr. Danehy's challenge to match boys
versus girls for the science field trip wasn't such a
bad idea after all.

Next in line, Madison came face-to-face with an

e-mail that never should have been there. Who was 1234Gotcha? The subject "XXX RATED" was like a flashing neon light that said, "You Shouldn't Open Me." Sometimes Madison was curious about e-mails that she knew she *shouldn't* open. But she resisted. As Gramma Helen always said, "Curiosity killed the cat."

Madison didn't want any dead cats.

Delete.

Next she saw that Boop-Dee-Doop, the online clothing store, had sent a ten-dollars-off coupon for any upcoming purchase. The only trouble with that offer was that Mom had decided not to buy any new clothes for a while. Madison knew she wouldn't be using it before the expiration date.

Delete.

Finally Madison read a quick e-mail from Dad. He'd actually just sent it while she'd been online.

```
From: JeffFinn
To: MadFinn
Subject: Love You
Date: Mon 26 Mar 2:49 PM
How are you? Work has been off the
wall. Staying in Boston again for a
long weekend, and I sure do miss my
little girl. Taking the train home
tomorrow.

I'm having Stephanie over for
```

dinner, too. It'll be fun with the
three of us!

Love, Dad

P.S. Why did the doughnut maker
stop working? Because he was fed up
with the hole business! LOL.

Madison could never get used to Dad's lame
jokes, but she had gotten used to the fact that
Stephanie seemed to go *everywhere* Dad went these
days. They'd been dating so long now that Dad
didn't even ask for Madison's permission to invite his
"girlfriend" over when Madison was coming over,
too.

Thankfully, Mom wasn't dating *anyone*.

Madison's computer bleeped. She had an Insta-
Message.

<Bigwheels>: Hello r u really there?

Madison was so surprised to hear from her keypal
in the middle of the school day. It was earlier in the
day where Bigwheels lived, in Washington, all the
way across the country.

<MadFinn>: Bigwheels! Ur at school?
<Bigwheels>: Yes but I'm in the
    computer lab & TAW

45

```
<MadFinn>: how r u?
<Bigwheels>: TERRIBLE! I had a fight
    w/my BFF Lainie
<MadFinn>: oh no!!!!
<Bigwheels>: GGN—write to me l8r
<MadFinn>: ok bye
```

Madison glanced over at the clock and panicked a little. Mom could walk in any moment! She needed to print out her research pages now so Mom could get on the computer when she came back home. Usually Mom worked in the evenings before and after dinner.

Madison signed off bigfishbowl.com, but she stayed online. Then she booted up her disk from the school media center and reread what she'd typed up earlier. She was very glad that she'd ended up choosing Amelia Earhart as her paper's topic.

While the research pages were printing, Madison skipped around to some other search engines. The English paper wasn't the only project weighing on her mind. She still needed to look for information for her science trip.

Up in the corner of the screen, Madison noticed the familiar Favorites icon. That gave her a great idea. Mom surfed the Web a lot—and she always saved all the important science and educational Web sites for easy access.

Madison clicked Mom's Favorites icon, and a

shorthand list of handy-dandy Web site names appeared.

```
Movies R Us
Science Playground
Teacher Plans/Lessons
PBS
Into the Wild
Date-O-Magic
Film Center USA
```

Madison stopped and scrolled backward.
Date-O-Magic?

She clicked the link for that site and watched slowly, surprised, as a home page she never expected to see came up on the screen. A banner scrolling across the top said, "Meet the Man of Your DREAMS. . . ."

Date-O-Magic wasn't about science or education. This was an online *dating* service.

Madison's stomach did a major flip-flop.

She hit the power key and watched the screen turn black with a sizzle.

Chapter 5

Tuesday afternoon Fiona had soccer practice and Aimee had a private dance lesson, so Madison came home alone after school. Mom wasn't home again, but Billy was back working on the roof and chimney. Madison ignored him.

After a quick snack, Madison logged on to Bigfishbowl.com. She was very surprised to find Bigwheels online again in the middle of the day.

```
<Bigwheels>: Hi. I'm at home today.
<MadFinn>: U ok?
<Bigwheels>: I have the flu
<MadFinn>: Yuck-o. Sorry
<Bigwheels>: No fun being sick
<MadFinn>: So start at the beginning
    and tell me EXACTLY what happened
    w/ your BFF
```

```
<Bigwheels>: Lainie and I are not
     speaking we had a major fight
<MadFinn>: but what happened? she's
     ur BFF!!
```

Madison Finn blinked at the flashing computer
screen. Bigwheels was slow in responding. Was her
online keypal having a BFF mini-meltdown?

```
<Bigwheels>: yeah Lainie WAS my BFF
     but now she's acting like a
     supersnob
<MadFinn>: How?
<Bigwheels>: yesterday she said she
     was too busy to hang out after
     school & then I saw her talking
     to this OTHER girl after school
     and all I can say is that she is
     SUCH a major liar and TLGO and O
     and O
<MadFinn>: bummer
<Bigwheels>: she's acting all weird
     and secretive
<MadFinn>: you'll prob make up
     sooner than soon
<Bigwheels>: thanks I hope so but I
     don't know she is being so
     different than b4 we NEVER had
     n e secrets w/each other
<MadFinn>: I think maybe my mom is
     keeping a big secret from me and
```

49

```
      she NEVER keeps secrets from me,
      either
<Bigwheels>: no way—what?
<MadFinn>: well I think she's dating
      again
<Bigwheels>: WOW
<MadFinn>: what am I supposed 2 do?
```

Bigwheels was slow in responding again.

```
<MadFinn>: BIGWHEELS r u there?
<Bigwheels>: AFK
<MadFinn>: What's wrong?
<Bigwheels>: My mom was yelling 4
      me and I have to go to the
      doctor now—I'll send u an e-mail
      later—write back
```

Madison logged off. She was disappointed that she and her keypal were cut off before she could get some good advice. Even worse, now that Madison had brought up the subject, she couldn't get *Date-O-Magic* out of her mind.

"Wanna go *o-u-t*?" she cried to Phinnie. She held out his leash.

It was almost four o'clock, and a walk outside would clear her head. Maybe Aimee was home from dance class? If she was, Aimee and Madison could walk their dogs together. Phin loved Aimee's basset hound, Blossom. It would be the perfect distraction.

She left a note for Mom on the front door saying that she went to Aimee's house.

When Madison arrived at the Gillespies' house, however, Madison found her BFF's mom instead of her BFF.

"Oh, Maddie, I'm sorry," Mrs. Gillespie said when she opened the front door. "Aimee's still at her ballet lesson."

Madison shifted from foot to foot. "Bummer," she mumbled. "Well, see ya."

Mrs. Gillespie opened the screen door wider. "Do you want a snack?" she asked. "I just made some homemade granola."

Aimee's mother was a health nut. She made almost every recipe in her kitchen with wheat germ or tofu. Madison wasn't a *huge* fan of health-food cooking, however. She made a sour face.

"Whoopsie! I forgot." Mrs. Gillespie chuckled to herself. "You don't like that all-natural stuff."

"But it was really nice of you to ask," Madison said. "I just came over to take Phin for a walk with Blossom and Aimee, but it can wait for another—"

"Why don't *we* go together?" Mrs. Gillespie interrupted. "Let me grab Blossom's leash."

Before Madison could even respond, Mrs. Gillespie had disappeared to find Blossom. Madison sat down on their front steps. Phin was sniffing everything he could sniff. He smelled hound.

Often, when Mom was out of town, Madison

51

would stay overnight for a day or longer with the Gillespies. Mrs. Gillespie knew how to say all the right things if Madison was feeling blue. Maybe she'd know what to say today?

As they walked the dogs around Blueberry Street and Ridge Road, Madison tried to get up the courage to ask a few questions about what she'd discovered on her mom's computer. Mrs. Gillespie would know why Mom was on that Web site, wouldn't she?

"Mrs. Gillespie, have you ever heard of Date-O-Magic?" Madison blurted.

Aimee's mother barely blinked an eye. "Date-O-*what*?" she asked.

"Date-O-MAGIC," Madison repeated, a little louder for emphasis. "It's some kind of Web site."

"Never heard of it," Mrs. Gillespie said. "Doesn't sound like something a seventh grader should really be looking at, though—"

"No, I wasn't," Madison said. "I think Mom was."

Mrs. Gillespie put her hand gently on Madison's shoulder. "Isn't that her business?" she asked.

"I guess. But I found out by accident, and now I know what's going to happen. My mom is going to start dating, just like my dad," Madison said. "She's going to start dating some strange guy from the Internet and then—"

"Hold on," Mrs. Gillespie said calmly. "She wouldn't

date anyone without telling you about it. You know that."

Madison sighed. "But what if she *is* dating someone?" she asked.

"You know, Maddie," Mrs. Gillespie said. "I think maybe the person you should be talking to about this is your—"

"Mom," Madison grumbled. "Yeah, I know."

"Yes," Mrs. Gillespie said. "You should talk to your mom *and* your dad about these feelings. Especially about the dating. I know it can't be easy dealing with everything that's happened since last year. We've discussed this before."

They had talked a lot about dealing with change. Sometimes when Madison slept over at Aimee's house, she'd spend as much time talking to Aimee's mother as she spent talking to Aimee. Mrs. Gillespie couldn't help but be supportive 24/7.

From the sidewalk, they watched Phin and Blossom sneak behind some bushes. Mrs. Gillespie turned to Madison and chuckled. "The real question here is, 'How do we feel about *them* dating?'"

Madison giggled. Phin was chasing Blossom around so much, their leashes got tangled together. Mrs. Gillespie leaned over to give Madison a hug, and Madison couldn't help but squeeze back—hard.

When they arrived back at the Gillespie house, Aimee was inside. They hung out together in

Aimee's room so Phin could have some extra playtime with Blossom. Aimee showed Madison the picture she'd finally selected for the ballet programs.

Around five o'clock, Mom called the Gillespies' and asked Madison to hurry home. Dad was back from Boston. He was coming by to pick Madison up for dinner.

On the way out, Madison waved to Aimee's brother Roger, who was standing in the driveway to fix something under his car's hood. Roger was the nicest guy on the planet. If she were just a little bit older, Madison thought, maybe she could go out on a date with *him*.

Whereas Aimee thought Roger was perpetually annoying, Madison thought he was smart, cute, *and* funny—not the traits of most boys at Far Hills Junior High these days. Especially not Hart Jones.

Madison paced by the front door, watching as the sun began its slow drop down in the sky. Dad and Stephanie were on their way over to pick Madison up for dinner.

"He's *late* again?" Mom called out from the kitchen.

It was now six-twenty.

Madison strolled into the kitchen. "Quit picking on him, Mom. He isn't *always* late," Madison rushed to Dad's defense. "He's just superbusy."

"Aren't we all?" Mom laughed.

54

Madison shrugged. "Can we just change the subject, please?"

She collapsed onto a kitchen chair and rested her head on the table.

"Honey bear, did you use my computer last night?" Mom asked.

"Huh?" Madison nodded, lifting her head. "Yeah. Why?"

Was Mom able to see that Madison had surfed to Date-O-Magic?

"Well, you left the printer on," Mom said. "Next time be careful, okay?"

Madison wanted to blurt, "Why don't *you* tell me what's going on with Date-O-Magic, huh?" But she didn't. She wasn't ready to bring up that subject with her mom yet.

The reality of Dad and Mom *both* seeing other people made Madison a little dizzy. Somewhere in her heart, she still harbored the teeniest of hopes that maybe (just maybe) her parents would reunite.

Dad showed up when Madison and Mom were still talking. He punched the doorbell three times in a row. Madison kissed her mom good-bye.

On the way to the car, Dad gave Madison a giant squeeze. Stephanie was waiting for them in the front seat.

"Hiya, Maddie," she said as Madison climbed into the backseat. "What's going on?"

Madison had grown to like Dad's girlfriend a lot,

except at certain times like now, when she had to ride in the backseat. Madison felt like a third wheel. She watched the scenery flash by and only answered with one- or two-syllable responses.

"Yuh."

"Uh-huh."

"Yep."

They didn't go to Dad's loft for dinner, which was a huge disappointment for Madison. Dad used to cook all the time, but since he'd been dating Stephanie, he had all but stopped cooking for Madison's visits. And even on the rare occasions when he *did* cook, Dad's most special recipes (namely, the ones Madison adored) weren't on the main menu.

They went to an Italian bistro, a new restaurant on the border of Far Hills and another town along the river called Burkeville. Dad stopped to let a valet park the car as everyone hopped out. It was a super-fancy place. Their table had a view of the waterfront.

Madison gazed at the reflection of different-colored lights, with a rainbow of blues, yellows, whites, and pinks glimmering off the water and the sides of boats. She was in a faraway fog.

"How's school?" Dad asked Madison in the middle of salad, trying to pull her back into the table's conversation.

"School's cool," Madison said with a mouthful of

lettuce. "Except for science class. We have this field trip coming up tomorrow, and I don't really know what to expect."

Stephanie asked a string of questions about where they were going and what they'd be seeing. She couldn't believe they'd be competing boys versus girls.

"That's outrageous, Jeff," Stephanie said. "You really should talk to the principal. Isn't that sexism or something like that?"

Madison grinned at Stephanie's enthusiasm. "Well, the trip's tomorrow, so it's too late to change anything."

Dad chuckled. "I say, 'You go, girl!'"

"Oh, Dad." Madison groaned. "How embarrassing."

Stephanie laughed. "Well, beat the boys, then," she whispered to Madison.

Dad gave Stephanie a kiss after she said that.

The spaghetti came to the table late, and the evening seemed to drag on. By the time they had paid the check and got into the car heading home, Madison felt her eyes getting heavy. Today had been overly busy just like all the rest of the days of the week.

Zzzzzzzzzzzzzzz.

No sooner had Madison dozed off than Dad leaned into the backseat to help her out of his car. "C'mon, sweetie," he said. Stephanie whispered her good-byes, too.

A groggy Madison grunted hello to Mom when she walked inside. From her office, Mom could only manage a limp hello herself. She looked drained, too. Mom obviously had spent the entire evening at her computer, compiling editing data and fact checking for one of her film documentaries. There was a half-eaten TV dinner on Mom's work desk.

"You look beat, Mom," Madison said.

"Mmmm. How was dinner?" Mom asked. "*You* look beat, too."

Madison shrugged. She *was* tired—too tired to talk. Kissing Mom's head, she dashed away for the makeshift bedroom in the den. Madison's real room was still off-limits for sleeping.

In the den, Madison found her laptop computer lying open on the sofa, still plugged in and fully charged. She clicked the space bar, and the screen lit up.

As the computer buzzed on, Madison felt her own inner batteries recharge, too. And so she and her second wind headed immediately into her private files.

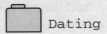 Dating

    I'm having a crisis, and it has to do
with a four-letter word that I'm beginning
to detest:
    D-a-t-e.
    I wish I could say the crisis about

the word *date* is because three different boys want to ask me out. HA HA HA LOL—that isn't even close.

It's Mom and Date-O-Magic that has me in knots.

AND I can't talk to Dad about it because he'll just back up Mom like he always does.

AND Dad is being so sweet to Stephanie these days (I think he *loves* her, but let's save that for another file) and I feel weird talking about Mom in front of Stephanie. Does it hurt her feelings? She acts all normal when I talk about Mom, but I know what she's *really* thinking. . . .

I totally can't talk to my friends about any of this, either, because it would be way, way too embarrassing. They just don't get it. Aimee's and Fiona's parents have both been married forever. They think I'm a super-worrywart. Fiona even says I'm *lucky* since one day I'll probably have four parents instead of two. Lucky?

Rude Awakening: Life with parents who go on dates is like watching a baseball game. You need to watch out for curveballs—and you definitely need to keep score.

Madison hit SAVE and closed the Dating file. She realized that she was probably jumping the gun about Mom's dating life, but she didn't care.

In addition to keeping herself busy with school,

after school, friends, the computer, volunteering, and the flute, Madison had one more thing to add to her superbusy to-do list of life.

Keep an eye on Mom.

Chapter 6

Phinnie leaped onto the couch and pressed his little pug paws into Madison's sides and nuzzled her neck with his very wet nose. Madison rolled off the couch, nearly taking the dog with her. It was almost seven o'clock, and she needed to dress fast.

Today was the BIG date she'd been waiting for all week: the science field trip.

"Have you seen my sneakers, Mom?" Madison yelled downstairs. She pulled on a pair of striped socks and painter's pants. "And my light-blue T-shirt? The one with the angel on the front?"

Mom came to the bottom of the stairs and growled. "I wish you wouldn't yell, Madison. I haven't even had my coffee yet."

"Sorry," Madison said a little more softly. "Have you seen my angel shirt?"

"Yes," Mom said. "It's in the laundry."

Madison wanted to kick herself for not planning her outfit the night before. Now she had no idea what top to wear. She pulled on a plain yellow shirt with embroidery around the sleeves and neck and pulled her hair into a ponytail.

"Mirror, mirror, on the wall . . ." she mumbled to herself in the bathroom mirror. She posed sideways and front ways and decided it would have to work. It was the only shirt that really went with the pants, anyway.

Downstairs, Mom was in the kitchen, making Madison a peanut-butter sandwich with a little plastic bag of chips on the side. Mom still looked groggy, too, which meant she'd been up very late working in her office.

"Do you like this shirt?" Madison asked. "I mean, do you think this is a good field trip outfit?"

Mom rubbed her eyes. "Sure, honey bear." She gave Madison a kiss on the head.

"I'm serious, Mom," Madison said. "What do you think?"

"I think you look fine," Mom said, pouring a coffee refill.

"Fine? Oh no, it's *ugly*, isn't it?" Madison blurted. "I should change, right? I'm going to go and change." And just like that, Madison turned around and headed back upstairs.

After three more outfit tests, she finally picked

the winning combination: faded jeans and an orange Boop-Dee-Doop T-shirt with a panda bear on the front. It even matched her striped socks.

Madison raced to get her bag together so she could meet Aimee and walk to school early. The buses were supposed to leave by eight-thirty, and Madison and Aimee wanted to get good seats.

The school yard was half full by the time they arrived. Madison didn't see Fiona anywhere, but Chet was loafing around by the fence with Egg, Drew, Hart, and Dan. The boys looked like a team. They were all dressed in the same kind of baggy pants with faded T-shirts and baseball caps. It was like *their* field trip uniform.

"Hey, Finnster!" Hart yelled when he saw Madison.

His voice was amplified by the stillness of the morning air.

She wanted to run away, but she waved. That stupid nickname sounded so wonderful when Hart said it.

Egg was snickering, as usual. He made a face at Madison, and she stopped waving right away.

"I don't know why we rushed over," Aimee complained. "Only half the seventh grade is here so far."

Lindsay ran up to both of them. She had on a droopy hat and overalls. "Hey, guys," she said. Another two girls from their class followed Lindsay, but they didn't say much. One of them had a cast on her arm.

Across the yard, the teachers were congregating in small groups, looking over their lists and clipboards. They looked funnier than funny in *their* field trip garb. Mr. Danehy wore blue jeans that looked like they'd been ironed.

"I can't believe you have him for science." Aimee chuckled. "My teacher is so much cooler than him."

"She's also like a century younger than he is," Madison said.

They were talking about Ms. Ripple, another science teacher, who acted more like a friend than a teacher to her students. Kids in class liked her because she always graded on a curve and she hardly ever gave homework. Aimee wasn't even given a prep sheet for the day's trip, while Madison had two pages of questions to explore and answer.

As they stood there in small groups, talking, the buses finally pulled into the parking lot. The school's principal, Mr. Bernard, came outside the school to wish everyone in seventh grade a happy field trip.

"Don't *they* make a good couple," Aimee teased, looking over at Mr. Danehy and Ms. Ripple.

Madison almost laughed, but then she swallowed her laughter. She had a terrible thought about Mom going on a date with someone like Mr. Danehy. What if her mom dated a science teacher from Date-O-Magic? Madison couldn't deal with that, especially not a date with *her* teacher.

"Well, hello, there!" Fiona said, dashing across the school yard. She had her hair pulled up with barrettes and her new glasses.

"You look so good!" Aimee said.

"I think the frames are cool," Fiona said. "The guy at the store said they made me look intelligent."

"He said *that*?" Aimee teased.

Fiona put her hands on her hips. "Yes, he did!"

"They are cool," Madison said. With or without glasses, Fiona always looked like a model to her.

"So do you think I look any smarter, Maddie?" Fiona giggled.

Madison giggled right back. "Total genius."

"Whassup?" Egg said. He came over as soon as he saw Fiona standing there. "Nice glasses, Fiona."

Fiona grinned. "Yeah. Do you really like them?"

"Sure," Egg said, acting doofier than doofy.

After he walked away, Madison turned to Aimee and Aimee turned to Madison. They were thinking the same thing.

"What happened to Egg?" Aimee asked.

"Yeah," Madison said. "Normally if he saw one of us wearing glasses, he'd call us four eyes or something. But not you, Fiona. . . ."

Fiona blushed, and Aimee gave her a squeeze.

One of the teachers blew a whistle and asked the kids to line up in three lines for the three buses to the nature center. Fiona and Lindsay paired up behind Madison and Aimee. Just behind them, all

65

the boys in their group lined up. Hart was three feet from Madison, but she barely looked his way.

From nowhere, Poison Ivy Daly appeared with her drones following right behind. They cut to the front of the line. Madison noticed what Ivy was wearing. She couldn't believe her enemy had on the same angel T-shirt that Madison had almost worn this morning. That was a closer-than-close call.

Kids piled into the trio of buses with their groups of friends. Everyone squished in two to a seat. Egg thought he was being funny when he sat on top of Hart and Chet in their row. They just kicked him off.

"What's going on back there?" Mr. Danehy's voice boomed.

Egg scrambled to sit in his real seat near Drew. Aimee could barely contain her laughter. Bus chaos had started, and they'd only just boarded. Madison turned around to see that Ivy had an entire seat all to herself in the back of the bus.

Of course, Ivy never played by the rules.

The bus driver was a round, short man with red hair and a mustache. He growled at the kids, "Keep it down!" and everyone hushed up.

It didn't last long, though. The moment the bus gassed up and got going, everyone began murmuring. The noise rose slowly as the buses pulled out of the Far Hills Junior High parking lot and onto the main road.

And they're off!

Since Mr. Danehy had taken his seat way up at the front of the bus, Chet took the opportunity to do one of his Danehy imitations. Everyone was laughing, even Ivy. Egg stood up again and wobbled as if he'd fall over into Hart again, too. It seemed fine until the bus jerked onto an on-ramp on its way to the highway.

Egg went flying and landed on someone else's lap for real.

Madison.

"Get off me!" Madison yelled.

Fiona was laughing so hard, her glasses almost fell off her face. Aimee had her hands covering her mouth. Even Lindsay laughed.

Egg was stuck.

"I SAID, GET OFF ME!" Madison screamed.

Mr. Danehy turned around right away when he heard *that*. He stood up and marched to the back, yanking Egg from Madison's lap and placing him back in his own seat.

"Young man," Mr. Danehy grumbled. He didn't know Egg's full name. "Keep it calm back here or you'll be sitting next to me."

Hart smacked Egg on the back from the seat behind. "Nice going, Walt." Sometimes kids would use Egg's real name to irritate or make fun of him.

Egg shot a look toward Madison. "Nice going, *Finnster*," he said.

Madison stuck out her tongue at him.

"QUIT IT!" someone else yelled from the back of the bus.

A bunch of kids whipped around to see Joanie, one of Ivy's drones, kneeling on her seat with her hands in the air. She was leaning forward, trying to grab something one of the boys had stolen from her.

Chet tossed something to Drew. He held it over his head. Madison could see that it was a small bottle of nail polish. It looked a lot like the color Aimee had painted onto her nails.

"GIVE IT!" Joanie yelled.

Mr. Danehy didn't hear them, though—yet.

"Don't be a loser," Ivy said. "Give it back, Drew."

But Drew tossed it into the row in front of him. It landed in Hart's lap.

"GIVE IT!" Joanie yelled again.

Hart quickly passed the bottle to Egg.

Before Egg could pass it along to anyone else, Mr. Danehy turned around. Luckily he didn't see anything wrong.

Ivy got up and stood in front of Egg's seat. "Hand it over," she said.

Egg crossed his arms and made a face. "I don't think so." He held the bottle to the side where she couldn't reach.

Unfortunately for him, he reached out directly in front of Madison. She leaned over and grabbed the bottle. Then she handed it to Ivy.

"Traitor!" Egg said to Madison, standing up. "What did you do that for?"

"Do what?" Madison said, acting like she didn't know what was going on.

Meanwhile Mr. Danehy had turned around again. This time he heard and saw everything. He rushed over and grabbed Egg by the collar.

"Get your things, young man," Mr. Danehy said. Egg would have a brand-new, front-row seat for the remainder of the bus ride—right next to Mr. Danehy. While he was standing there, Mr. Danehy confiscated the bottle of nail polish, too.

"I'm going to get you for this, Maddie," Egg said. Madison looked the other way.

Ivy glanced at Hart before returning to her own seat. "I didn't know you played stupid games," she said, acting all huffy.

Score one for Ivy.

Sometimes it seemed like Madison's best enemy had an answer for everything.

Hart didn't seem to care one bit about Ivy's comment, as obnoxious as it was. He turned backward and gave Chet a high five. But boys always stuck together like that.

After ten more minutes of loud talk and commotion, their bus pulled onto a dirt road. A large sign read FAR HILLS NATURE TRAIL AHEAD. Another sign, a few feet beyond that, read SLOW DOWN.

As the bus slowed, it bumped along more, and

everyone held on to the seats in front of them. Lindsay said she felt like throwing up. But strangely, Madison felt calmer than calm.

It was so quiet and green.

Once the bus stopped, everyone pushed and shoved to get out. Although they were sitting all the way in the back, Ivy and her drones acted like they deserved to get off the bus first. Fiona stepped in front of Ivy before she could go any farther.

Ivy tapped her foot and sighed loudly so everyone could hear. "Nice glasses," she said under her breath.

Fiona smiled. "Thanks, Ivy. I like them, too." Then she took an extra-long time getting her backpack and even let Lindsay go ahead. Ivy would have to wait. And wait. And wait some more.

Fiona was so good at getting revenge *quietly*.

"Way to go," Madison whispered as they got off the bus.

"That was inspired," Lindsay said.

Mr. Danehy blew a loud whistle, and a bunch of birds flew out of one tree. Everyone milling around outside the three buses shut up fast. They piled up their backpacks and lunch sacks by the nature center's main lodge. These would be retrieved later.

Egg wandered over to Hart, Chet, Drew, and Dan, who were standing next to Aimee and the other girls. He pointed his finger directly at Madison and said, "I'm going to get you!" Then he pinched Madison's arm.

Madison flinched. "Ouch," she cried.

Dan chuckled out loud. "Pinch him back, Maddie," he said.

But Hart stepped in between the two. "Give it a rest, Egg," he said. Then he turned around toward Madison so close, they were nose to nose.

And he smiled.

It wasn't a big deal. Just an ordinary smile. But Madison thought she felt her cheeks blush pink. Did anyone notice? She couldn't believe that suddenly an annoying Hart had turned crushable again. *Like that*.

A little part of her insides felt like they were melting.

Hart was still smiling.

Madison wasn't quite sure what she was *really* feeling in that moment, but she knew one thing for sure.

The boys versus girls field trip at the science center was going to be *way* more surprising than she—or anyone else—ever expected.

Chapter 7

"Who is *that*?" Aimee said, grabbing Madison's arm. They were staring at a tall, dark-haired guy dressed in green pants and a shirt with a Far Hills Nature Trails logo on the front.

"Whoa," Lindsay said, smirking. "Cuteness."

Even Fiona was interested. "He *is* cute."

He wore a badge that said MY NAME IS RANGER JIMMY, and Madison couldn't take her eyes off him, either. None of the girls could.

As luck would have it, he stood next to Ivy, who was doing her hair-flipping, look-at-me thing. But Jimmy directed his warm greeting to *everyone* in the group.

"Welcome to the park," he said in a sweet voice. "I'll be your field guide."

The boys made a hissing noise when Jimmy

started to speak. They were already kicking into goofball gear. One kid pumped his fist up into the air. "Wooo! Wooo!"

"Older guys are so much more mature," Ivy whispered. Her drones nodded. Madison and Aimee and the rest of the girls standing there heard it, too.

Score two for Ivy.

Everyone was flirting with the field guide. Madison knew that Jimmy could tell, but he didn't act weird or flirty at all. He explained that he was a college sophomore volunteering at the center during his days off from classes. He was a biology major because he loved animals. And he had a pet iguana.

Madison hung on his every word. They had so much in common, except for the iguana part.

"OKAY, KIDS," a booming voice interrupted Jimmy's talk.

Mr. Danehy came waddling over, barking in the same, loud, oddly unidentifiable accent he always spoke in class. "Girls, now you'll get together in one group. You'll be going around with Jimmy here. Boys, you gather over by that tree. Ranger Lester and I will escort you. Ah! Here he comes now."

Lester appeared through a door at the main gatehouse. He was dressed in safari clothes with stuff attached all over his belt. He had a long, grizzled beard that looked a little like a bird's nest. He clapped before he ever said anything.

Clap, clap.

"Well, hello there, young men," he said.

Clap, clap.

"Nature awaits us!" he said. "Are you pre-pared?"

"What's with this guy?" Madison heard Chet whisper to his friends. "How come we don't get some cute *girl* to lead our group?"

Madison was relieved to see that Aimee's science teacher, Ms. Ripple, would be walking around with them.

The boys split off toward one path; the girls headed to another.

"I'd like everyone to please treat this area care-fully," Jimmy said as they started to hike. "The crea-tures and plant life need your special consideration. If you look over here, we have some rules to follow along the trail."

Madison saw a sign engraved on a giant log:

❖ BE CONSIDERATE OF OTHERS ALONG THE TRAIL
❖ DO NOT CLIMB ON FENCES OR RAILS
❖ NO LITTERING
❖ NO SMOKING
❖ DO NOT DISTURB THE HABITATS
❖ FIELD GUIDES MUST ACCOMPANY ALL LARGE GROUPS

A few feet farther along, Madison saw a larger sign with animal tracks painted all over it.

❖ TAKE NOTHING BUT MEMORIES
❖ LEAVE NOTHING BUT FOOTPRINTS

Jimmy pointed to the path. "We'll be traveling through some wooded areas, so please be sure to stay on the trails and beware of poison ivy."

Madison yelled out, "Ha!"

Aimee and Fiona snorted.

Luckily no one else knew what the laughter was all about.

"As I was saying," Jimmy continued. "We are guests in the home of the environment. So watch your steps."

Madison pulled her science-class checklist out of her bag. Ivy scurried over to see it.

"I left mine at home," Ivy said as she leaned over Madison's shoulder.

"Uh." Madison tried to say something else, but nothing came out.

"Take your own notes," Aimee snapped.

Ivy shot her a look. "Why don't you just butt out?"

"It's okay, Aim," Madison said. "We can share."

"Thanks," Ivy said, walking a little bit ahead of Madison. The drones had forgotten their checklists, so Madison would be sharing everything with them, too.

"Maddie," Aimee said, grabbing Madison's arm. "Who made Ivy queen?"

"We *are* on the same side," Madison said,

defending her actions. "We're all girls, right? And she and I are partners, so . . ."

"So *what*?" Aimee said.

Beating the boys at this contest had become the most important goal for Madison—even more important than getting even with Ivy.

The girl group followed Jimmy along the wooded path toward a clearing. Right away, Madison saw three of the items on the list. She checked them off.

```
Deer or raccoon tracks ✔
Spider's web ✔
Worm ✔
```

Jimmy pointed out that the woodland habitat was filled with creatures the class might not see at first glance. He showed everyone the underside of a green leaf and revealed a fuzzy caterpillar.

Madison checked that off her list.

"Look over there!" a girl from Ms. Ripple's science class shrieked. "SKUNK!"

Everyone squished closer together and let out a little whoop.

Jimmy chuckled. "I don't think you saw a skunk," he said. He wandered over to the spot where the girl had seen the black-and-white movement. A whirligig was sticking up out of the ground there. It was a wooden woodpecker whirling around in the wind.

"Give me a break," Ivy said. She raised her hand to ask a question. "What is *that* doing there?"

Jimmy smiled. "We have numerous whirligigs of birds placed throughout the center. They serve as markers along the trail in case visitors lose their way. You can follow the path toward the woodpecker, the cardinal, or the blue jay."

"Sort of like ski trails or something," Lindsay said.

"Exactly," Jimmy said, still smiling.

Lindsay quietly nudged Fiona. "Did you see that? He smiled at me."

"He smiles at *everyone*," Ivy said roughly. She pushed her way toward the front.

Madison wondered how the boys were doing on their walk through the woods. She imagined Chet and Hart getting into trouble—and Mr. Danehy chasing after them with a big stick. Other than a few snipes from Poison Ivy Daly, the girl group was mellower than mellow.

"Look at all the new flowers," Fiona said. There were purple and yellow flowers poking themselves up through the wet earth.

"Those are wild irises," Jimmy told Fiona and the rest of the group.

The group marched on together through fields of wildflowers, most of which were just starting to get very green after a long winter. Very few had any color because it was so early in the springtime.

Ms. Ripple gasped when she nearly stepped on a

slug. Someone else got overexcited when *two* lady-bugs landed on her at the same time.

Jimmy kept the group moving right along. "We're leaving the field habitat now," he announced, walking down a small hill. "Heading toward the duck pond habitat now. Everyone please stay together."

"Isn't he so cute?" Fiona whispered to Aimee and Madison.

"Look over there," Aimee said. She saw a mama duck and some ducklings nestled together in some high grass. "Now, *that* is even cuter!"

Lindsay laughed. "Quick, everyone! DUCK!"

Everyone in the group chuckled.

"We have swans around the pond, too," Jimmy explained. "I just don't see any in the water right now."

Madison had fallen to the back of the group. She was quickly scanning the area in all directions, checking off more items on her list. Ivy hurried over to make sure "their" list was coming along all right. She leaned over Madison's shoulder to see.

```
Duckling(s)  ✔
Pond weed  ✔
Lily pad(s)  ✔
Snail  ✔
```

Jimmy asked everyone in the group to take seats on a series of benches around the duck pond. He passed out crumbs for feeding the ducks. By the time Madison and Ivy arrived, they were able to grab a handful of crumbs, but unfortunately all the seats were filled.

Madison wandered over to a grassy slope and sat down. Ivy was following right behind her. She wanted to take a look at Madison's notebook.

"Oh!" Jimmy exclaimed. "I wouldn't sit down there, girls!"

But it was too late.

Madison stood up and examined the back of her pants.

Duck poop.

Ivy stood up slowly and spun around, too. "What? What is it?" she cried.

"Oh, gross." Joanie moaned. "It's all over your pants, too, Ivy—"

"DON'T say it!" Ivy snapped. She twisted around some more to assess the damage.

More duck poop.

Instead of getting grumpy about it, Madison got a case of the giggles. Then the whole girl group started to laugh hysterically.

Except Ivy.

"Stop laughing right now!" Ivy said, still trying to wipe the stuff off her pants. Unfortunately, she had a more stubborn stain than Madison's. It took three Handi Wipes and some pond water to get Ivy's pants clean.

"Girls," Ms. Ripple said. "We shouldn't laugh at Ivy or Madison's misfortunes."

But Aimee laughed even harder.

After the poop incident had died down, the group trudged through mud down another short path. They seemed to be heading back into the woods.

"I'm glad I wore my yuckiest sneakers," Fiona said. They had mud splatters all over them.

Aimee groaned, looking down at her own shoes, which were brand-new. "Well, mine are yucky *now*," she said dejectedly.

The woods came to a stop in the middle of the path, and the group found itself in an enormous clearing. Across another field, Madison saw boys playing Frisbee. Mr. Danehy was standing over by some picnic tables. Everyone seemed to be lounging around.

"Hey!" Aimee cried, running across the field. She ran over to Egg. "What have you guys been doing all morning? Playing games?"

"No way," Egg said. "We've been looking at plants and birds. Same as you."

"Did you go to the duck pond?" Lindsay asked.

Hart tossed his head. "Nope. Where's that?"

"We skipped that part of the tour," Drew said.

"How can you skip part of the tour?" Madison asked. "We all have to answer the same questions. Where was Mr. Danehy?"

"He doesn't know we skipped out," Egg said.

"How will you do your project now?" Aimee asked.

Drew shrugged. "How hard can it be?"

Wonk.

Madison was about to speak again when out of nowhere a flying disk crash-landed on her shoulder.

"Hey!" she cried. "That hurt."

Aimee quickly looked to see who had sent the Frisbee flying. A few yards away another group of boys was laughing.

"Those guys hit you on *purpose*," Fiona said. "Look at them."

Aimee put her hand on Madison's arm. "Are you okay, Maddie?"

Egg, Drew, Dan, Hart, and Chet started to snicker.

"Nice aim!" Egg called back to the boys.

Madison put her hands on her hips. "You're toast, Egg," she said. "I mean it. That goes for all boys everywhere!"

The rest of the girls nodded enthusiastically.

"What did *we* do?" Hart asked.

"Like you have to ask!" Aimee shouted.

"Maddie, those *other* guys are the ones who threw it," Dan said.

Madison rubbed her arm and frowned. "Ouch."

"Is everything okay over here?" Ms. Ripple asked.

"Maddie got hit with a Frisbee," Egg said. "But it was an accident."

"Are you hurt?" Ms. Ripple asked Madison.

"No." Madison shrugged, not wanting to get Egg or anyone else in trouble. "It's okay."

"It was the boys!" Lindsay said.

"Totally! The boys!" Aimee said.

The rest of the girls cheered. "YEAH! THE BOYS!" Madison sighed.

The Far Hills Junior High war of the sexes had officially begun.

As usual, Madison felt like she was in the middle of *everything*.

Chapter 8

At lunch time, Madison, Aimee, and Fiona sat down to eat with Egg, Drew, and Chet—just the way they did at their usual orange table in the cafeteria.

Normally Madison would be thrilled to sit near her friends and her crush, but today she felt the exact opposite. She looked up, down, everywhere to avoid making eye contact with the boys, especially Hart.

"Hey, let's see where the Frisbee smashed you, Maddie. Do you have a bruise yet?" Chet asked her. "Come on, pull up your sleeve."

"Stop being such a pest," Fiona said to her twin brother.

"How *is* your arm, Finnster?" Hart asked.

Even though Hart sounded 100 percent earnest, Madison ignored him and the other boys, too. This infuriated Egg. He tried everything he could do to grab Madison's attention, including opening his mouth when he'd chewed up some of his cheese sandwich. He went, "Ahhhhh," in her face. Dan stuffed two brownies into his mouth at once and looked over at Madison, too. "Uuuuuuuuh," he grunted, as though he were speaking in some secret boy code.

Fiona stood up with her hands on her hips. "Are you guys being supergross today or is it me?"

"It's *you*, Fiona!" Chet said.

Drew started laughing until he snorted milk out of his nose. He gave Chet a high five. Egg couldn't stop laughing, either. He shoved the rest of his cheese sandwich into his mouth all at once.

"Ewwwwwwww!" Aimee yelled. "You're all DISGUSTING!"

She jumped backward away from the picnic table, which sent her plastic bag of carrots flying everywhere. One soaring carrot pinged Madison on the head. She'd become a target for flying objects of all kinds today.

Some kids were sure that a food fight would break out, but it didn't. Aimee leaned over to pick up the carrot missiles one by one.

"What are you doing?" Egg yelled. "Leave them there, Aim. The birds will eat them or something."

"What are you talking about, Egg?" Fiona asked. Even *she* seemed a little annoyed now. She'd never,

84

ever raised her voice to her crush before now. "We can't litter—this is a park. What's your problem?"

"What's *your* problem?" Egg cracked. "Little Ms. Goody."

Chet nodded in agreement, as did Drew and Dan.

Fiona looked ready to *cry*. But then Ranger Lester approached their picnic table with hands raised.

Clap, clap.

"Attention, everyone! The teachers have decided that you will all head to the next activity together, not in groups of boys or girls. Jimmy, your teachers, and I will be joint leaders."

Clap, clap.

Madison raised her hand. "But—" she started to say.

"Yes?" Ranger Lester said, still clapping like a trained seal.

Madison shook her head and didn't say anything more. She figured it was better to ignore the boys rather than let herself feel pestered. Of course, the whole time the ranger stood there at the table, the boys had behaved *perfectly*. No cheese sandwich or brownie surprises.

"Well, then," Ranger Lester said, looking around the now quiet table. "Let's shake a leg, then, shall we?" And with that, he shook his leg.

It was the last straw.

From out of nowhere, Aimee let out a laugh. She was trying so hard not to react to the annoying boys, the snappish exchanges, and most of all to the very strange ranger. But she couldn't hold back anymore.

Lindsay stuffed an orange slice into her mouth so *she* wouldn't laugh. All the other boys and girls at the table muffled their giggles, too. Ranger Lester didn't have a clue about what was going on around him. He laughed along with everyone else.

Meanwhile Fiona glanced in the other direction because she still looked ready to burst into tears.

Madison put her arm through Fiona's as they stood up to move to their next location. "Egg didn't mean it, Fiona," she comforted her friend. "He's just being a show-off. I'm sure he still likes you."

"I'm not sure I like *him*," she said.

Everyone at the table got up and headed over toward the teachers, who were organizing kids into groups. Next stop was the butterfly house and the apiary, otherwise known as the bee house.

Madison figured that bees were the kind of pests she and everyone else could handle—unlike Egg, Drew, Hart, Chet, Dan, Ranger Lester, and the rest of the boys in the universe.

Most kids pushed together to get a close look at the nature center demonstrations using bees and butterflies. But Fiona just sat on a bench and said she wasn't in the mood for nature. She wasn't in the mood for *anything*. She didn't know why.

Madison sat down to help her BFF. She could hear

Jimmy explaining how the apiary and butterfly zone worked. He was speaking through a loudspeaker.

"I'd like everyone to meet Doug. He's our resident beekeeper and butterfly keeper," Jimmy announced.

Doug was dressed in a white outfit that looked like a sumo wrestler's space suit. Madison could see he wore gloves and a mask that covered his entire head. He lifted off the mask and waved.

"Doug is in charge of maintaining all of the butterfly trees as well as our three primary beehives," Jimmy continued. "We keep them in this special bee house so the bees can produce their honey at the right temperature."

"It may be good for bees, but I say it's too hot in here," Egg said.

Ms. Ripple said, "Shhhhh!"

"Of course the temperature inside is also regulated for our butterflies," Jimmy explained. "When caterpillars make the transformation to chrysalis and cocoon, they need warmth. They can also get protection from the sheltering plants and shrubs we have inside the butterfly house."

"Look!" Aimee had her body pressed up against the screen so she could get a better look at a tree that was filled with yellow, orange, and brown butterflies. "It looks like they have letters on their wings!" she cried.

Doug walked over to the tree and put one of the

butterflies on his index finger so he could show the group up close. "Doug is holding a monarch butterfly," Jimmy announced over the loudspeaker.

"It's so pretty!" Lindsay said. "And that one has blue on the wings. The spots look like eyes."

"That's correct," Jimmy said. "Those spots are a decoy for predators. Enemies *think* those are eyes."

Chet, Drew, and Joanie joked about two butterflies that looked like they were fighting over a flower. Ivy and Lindsay were even chatting. Madison noticed how the butterflies had somehow brought friends and enemies together.

Doug wheeled out a tall cabinet. Inside, more than a hundred butterflies were shown in different stages of development. The entire crowd of seventh graders let out an "Oooooooh." Doug pointed to one butterfly that had just escaped its chrysalis but hadn't yet opened its wet wings.

Mr. Danehy wandered around the room to make sure all the kids were behaving, paying attention, and, in the case of *his* students, checking items off their ultra-important class checklist.

"Don't you want to see the butterflies?" Madison asked Fiona.

She shook her head. "No," she said. "I don't feel so good."

"I thought you liked this stuff," Madison said. But Fiona looked away.

Ivy appeared and sat down on the bench next to

Madison. "Aren't you taking notes on this?" she asked.

"Oh," Madison said. "I forgot. I was just looking at—"

"This stuff has to be important," Ivy huffed. "What are we going to do if you don't have the right notes?"

"Why can't *you* take some notes, Ivy?" Fiona said.

"I don't think I was talking to you," Ivy said. She stood up and went over to her group of friends.

"Maybe Egg should go out with Ivy," Fiona said under her breath. "They're both creeps."

Madison smiled and went to get a better look behind the screen.

"Let's take a look at bees inside the nature center," Jimmy's microphone voice boomed.

Doug wheeled away the chrysalis cabinet and then stood in front of one giant box. He lifted its lid. A dozen bees danced around the top.

From inside the box, Doug pulled out a slat that had an open screen on it. When he held it up for everyone to see, more bees danced around his arms and head. The slat was where some of the bees were busy making honey in a section of honeycomb.

Doug lifted up the slat that held the queen bee. Now the worker bees were moving around a little bit more than usual. They'd covered his arm and mask.

"I'm glad that guy's in there and not me," a voice next to Madison said.

She looked over to see Hart standing there.

"Yeah," Madison muttered. Her chest thumped. She'd been so annoyed with him before now. But standing there, one on top of the other in a big huddle of seventh graders, she had renewed feelings of "like."

She liked the shirt he was wearing, she liked the way his hair was parted, and she liked the way his voice sounded.

"Sorry about the lunch table thing," Hart whispered.

Madison shrugged. "Whatever," she said, her chest still pounding a little. She didn't want to like him. After all, she was a girl and this was girls versus boys.

But one look at his brown hair and . . .

"See ya!" Madison spun around and headed back over to the bench where Fiona was sitting. She had to leave the scene before her crush feelings took over entirely.

"Aren't bees *bad*?" some kid yelled to Doug. He could hear questions through the glass, but it was Jimmy's loudspeaker voice that replied.

"Definitely *not*," Jimmy said. "Bees are necessary for all life. They pollinate flowers and other plants that are necessary for *our* survival. I'd say that's good—not bad."

"Well said," Ranger Lester's voice boomed. "I'd say bees are terribly misunderstood creatures."

When Madison found Fiona again, she looked pale.

"What's wrong?" Madison asked. "Are you still upset about Egg?"

Fiona shook her head. "Not really. I just feel a little weird." She started itching her arm and lifted up her sleeve to reveal a blotch of brown bumps.

"What happened there?" Madison asked.

Fiona looked like she had a dozen pimples, chicken pox, and a bad rash all at the same time. She removed her new glasses and handed them to Madison, who shoved them into a pocket in her bag.

"I don't feel so good," she told Madison again.

Fiona leaned backward onto the bench and collapsed.

"Fiona!" Madison cried.

Everyone turned to look.

Chapter 9

Chapter 9

"What's the matter?" Aimee asked, rushing over when she heard Madison scream.

"I can't—can't—breathe—" Fiona said. She lifted her head and rubbed her ears. "I feel sick. I feel—"

"Don't move," Madison told Fiona. She yelled at Aimee, "Go get a teacher!"

Madison tried to remember what she'd been taught at the animal clinic about responding to emergencies. She'd also taken a sixth-grade CPR course last year. Madison tried to remember all at once everything she'd ever learned.

Think fast. Stay calm. Get help.

"Ow-eee," Fiona said, stretching out her arm. It was swollen like a log. Her neck looked like it was starting to swell a teeny bit, too. Madison remembered reading in a book somewhere that when the neck swelled, it could close up someone's throat and stop breathing.

But she didn't want to panic.

"I—really can't—breathe—" Fiona could barely talk anymore.

Madison stroked her head gently. "Someone will be right here," she said. "Please just relax."

Aimee rushed back instantly with Ranger Lester and Mr. Danehy. A crowd of kids was gathering around the bench.

"I think she got stung, and maybe she's allergic to bees," Madison pronounced to everyone with authority.

Mr. Danehy leaned toward Fiona and gently felt her head for fever. "Help is on the way, Fiona. You'll be fine." He asked Madison to get up and step away, but she stayed.

Chet pushed his way in toward the bench. "Fiona!" he shouted. "Oh no! What happened?"

"Is she allergic to bees?" Ranger Lester asked him seriously.

Chet shrugged. "I don't know. She's allergic to rabbits, I think."

Jimmy dashed over. "The medical station is coming right now. I'd advise everyone to step back."

Ms. Ripple and Ranger Lester helped the seventh graders to file out of the butterfly and bee house. Madison, Chet, and Aimee stayed behind.

"I thought all the bees were supposed to stay behind that glass," Madison said.

93

Jimmy nodded. "They should," he said, looking back toward the room, where the hives had now been sealed up again. Doug the beekeeper was putting everything away so no more accidents would happen. No one was really sure how Fiona had gotten stung.

Aimee waited on the other side of the bench, tapping her feet. "What's going on?" she kept saying. "What's going on?" She and Chet stood shoulder to shoulder, watching as Fiona struggled to breathe.

A doctor and his assistant rushed in moments later. He leaned over and looked carefully on Fiona's arm, where he quickly located the bee's stinger. "Gotcha!" he said, pulling something out of his satchel. He started to scrape Fiona's skin.

"Why aren't you just pulling it out?" Madison asked.

"Because," he said, still scraping to make sure he'd gotten all the venom, "only by scraping do you stop the bee's body from pumping poison into its target. Otherwise the stinger keeps on stinging."

His assistant took Fiona's other arm for a blood-pressure reading. She read the result aloud. *Blood pressure wasn't dropping*. Madison knew that was good news. Everyone else breathed a little sigh of relief, too—until the doctor pulled out a big needle.

"What's *that* for?" Chet asked.

Mr. Danehy grabbed Chet by the arm and pulled

him off to the side. "Let's go call your mom and dad, okay?" he asked, sensing the boy's nervousness.

Chet nodded. "Is my sister going to DIE?" he asked.

Mr. Danehy threw his arm around Chet's shoulders. "Of course not," he said, leading him toward the door. "But we need to call your parents now. They'll need to pick you both up."

Madison watched the doctor ready the needle. "What's that?" she asked.

"Adrenaline," the doctor said. Gently he pushed the needle into Fiona's arm. "This will stop the swelling."

"You'll be fine, Fiona," Madison whispered.

Aimee was sniffling.

"I'd like to take her over to the infirmary now," the doctor said to his assistant, raising Fiona up off the bench. Jimmy and Ranger Lester helped lift Fiona onto a stretcher.

"Is your infirmary for animals *and* people?" Madison asked.

"You sure do ask a lot of questions," the doctor said, smiling. "I like that. And yes, it is an infirmary for people *and* critters. We usually get a lot more problems with them than us."

Madison wished she could see it. Was it anything like the clinic at the Far Hills Animal Shelter, where she liked volunteering?

"What's going on *now*?" Aimee asked Madison as a man carefully wheeled Fiona away.

"They're helping her. She's going to be fine," Madison said.

"Oh my God," Aimee said, now breaking into tears completely. "How can you be so calm? She's swelling up like a balloon!"

Madison and Aimee followed the doctors and Fiona out of the apiary and butterfly house. As they exited, the entire seventh grade swarmed after Madison with questions.

"Did you see the bee that stung her?"

"Does Fiona hate bees?"

"Do we have to finish the field trip now?"

Madison shrugged. She didn't know the answers to any of *those* questions. Where was Mr. Danehy? Where was Jimmy?

Egg poked his way through a group of kids. Hart was right behind him.

"Did you save her life?" Egg asked Madison.

"You did save her life, didn't you?" Hart said. He sounded impressed.

Madison frowned. "I didn't do anything special."

"YES, YOU DID!" Aimee said. She looked at Egg directly. "While you guys were wasting time making stupid comments, Maddie was doing something important."

"Aimee," Madison contested. "I wasn't doing anything really—"

"I am still so worried," Aimee said to Madison as they lined up together again. "Should we be in there with her? Are you absolutely sure she's going to be okay?"

Madison nodded and smiled. "Of course."

The teachers blew a whistle, and all the seventh graders got back into their designated groups. With more than an hour left on the field trip, the class had to move right along to the next activity. The only faculty member who remained missing was Mr. Danehy, who stayed inside the nature center's infirmary with Chet and Fiona. He was waiting for Mr. and Mrs. Waters to arrive. The rest of the teachers and guides led everyone over to another lodge on the property of the nature center.

Jimmy made an announcement. "Okay, everyone," he said. "For the remainder of your time here, I'd like to invite you into our nature center gift shop."

Madison raised her hand. She was ready to volunteer right now. But Jimmy didn't see her at first.

"What are you doing?" Aimee asked, pulling Madison's arm out of the air.

"I think I might become a volunteer here," Madison said, trying to raise her arm again.

"Maddie," Lindsay said. "You were just talking this morning on the bus about how busy you are."

"Yeah," Aimee said. "You don't have time to volunteer at the animal shelter *and* here *and* do all your work. What planet are you on?"

"I can find time," Madison argued. "I know I'm busy. But I really want to do this. It's a great place."

"You just want to do it because Jimmy is Mr. Cute," Lindsay teased.

"Not true," Madison said. She giggled. "Well, only a little true."

They trio laughed together as they entered the gift shop.

Standing by the display of stuffed animals, Madison bumped into Ivy—literally. Ivy sneered.

"Walk much?" she said, turning away. Ivy's drones, who were standing there, sneered, too.

"Who does she think she is?" Joanie asked. "Florence Nightingale or something?"

They all laughed.

"Who is Florence Nightingale?" Aimee whispered to Lindsay. She softly explained that Florence Nightingale had been a nurse who helped soldiers during war.

"I'm actually writing an English paper on her," Lindsay said. "Ask me anything and I bet I can tell you."

"Oh, maybe another time," Aimee said. "Did I tell you guys that I'm writing mine on Isadora Duncan? She was a dancer."

Madison was reminded that she still hadn't finished *her* Women's History Month paper. Maybe her friends were right. Volunteering for the nature center wasn't a good idea after all. She *did* have homework that was late, other commitments with Mrs. Wing, flute lessons (and she'd hardly even practiced for the next one), and a bunch of other stuff.

She was busier than busy. Her Calendar Girl agenda was booked.

Madison Finn was busy as a *bee*, in fact.

Inside the gift shop, Madison used her allowance to buy a butterfly puzzle. She was thinking it might be a nice thing to give to Fiona after she recovered from her terrible bee sting. It was also on sale for only five dollars—exactly the amount she had in her bag.

Outside the gift shop, Mr. Danehy rejoined the group with his camera in hand. He wanted the classes to pose together for a field trip photo. Everyone stood next to a cardinal-red whirligig.

"This isn't the same without Fiona," Aimee said.

"Or Chet," Drew said.

But everyone said, "Cheese," and posed, anyway.

The field guides waved good-bye as the kids headed for the buses back to Far Hills Junior High. Jimmy stopped to pull Madison aside.

"I just wanted to say," Jimmy told her, "that you were very brave in there. You really helped your friend and all of us. The doctor wanted me to thank you personally. You and your friends."

Madison blushed like she always did when a guy stood so close.

"Tanks," she mumbled. "I mean, thanks."

Jimmy put his hand on her shoulder. "Thank *you*. Take good care of your friend now, okay? You should both come back to see us again."

Madison nodded like one of those plastic heads you put in the back window of a car. She was swooning inside, twice as much as she'd been earlier in the day while standing next to Hart. She hurried onto the bus, waving good-bye to Jimmy the entire time.

"What did he say?" Aimee and Lindsay asked as soon as Madison had taken her seat.

"He thanked me," she said. "He thanked me *personally*." She said the last part a little louder so Ivy could hear a few rows back. Madison could tell Ivy was eavesdropping, and she wanted to give her something really good to hear.

"He was a fox," Lindsay said.

"Megafox," Aimee said.

"And he's all mine," Madison said, giggling.

She turned back around to see her friends giggling, too. Unfortunately, she could also see Hart Jones. He wasn't giggling at all.

Madison stared out the window to avoid his stares, or what she thought were his stares. He could have just been looking in her general direction, right? She wasn't sure.

The bus driver passed another sign on the way out of the nature preserve with its familiar message:

"Let's get out of here!" some boy yelled from the back of the bus. A few other kids yelled in agreement. Madison could hear most boys in the back getting rambunctious just like they had that morning. Mr. Danehy voiced his loud disapproval.

Not *everyone* was acting dumb, though. Madison heard Drew say something about hoping that Fiona was okay. That was nice, Madison thought—*for a boy.*

Egg's voice could be heard above the rest, as usual. "I got stung by a bee on my foot once!" he said. "I went to the emergency room, and it hurt so bad."

"Me too!" Hart said. "I actually bumped into a whole beehive once. What happened to me was way worse than what happened today—"

"Who asked *you*?" Ivy Daly said.

Madison felt herself smile when she heard that, even if it was super-obnoxious.

Score another one for Ivy.

Madison's mind was abuzz. She couldn't wait to get home and open a new file to record all of today's adventures. She wanted to make a final plan of how she and her science partner, Ivy, and the rest of the girls could beat *all* the boys in Mr. Danehy's science class this week.

Sometimes even enemies had to come together and save the day.

Chapter 10

"Mom? MOM!" Madison yelled when she walked in the front door of her house. Phin rushed to the door, fanny wriggling.

"Rowrrooooooo!" he barked, sliding on the wood floors. He chased his tail around in circles and then made a mad dash for the living room. For the next few minutes he sped around the first floor, ears and tail wagging.

"Phinnie!" Madison said. But he didn't stop. "Mom, are you home?"

She wandered into the kitchen to grab a juice box.

"Madison!" Mom exclaimed as soon as she'd entered the room. "I didn't hear you come in. I was wondering what was going on with Phinnie running all around the house like a mad dog. . . ."

Madison stood as still as a statue, her mouth open.

Mom was sitting in the kitchen with a stranger.

A man stranger.

"You look as pale as a ghost," Mom said, standing up to feel Madison's forehead. "Oh, my goodness, what's happened?"

"Huh?" Madison said. "Who are *you*?" she added, looking directly at the stranger.

"This is Paul," Mom said, oozing sweetness. "He's a friend from work."

"Oh," Madison said. She wondered if Mom was telling the truth.

Was this guy from work or was he really from Date-O-Magic?

"Hey, there," Paul said in a low, low voice. He sounded like a DJ from the radio station Madison liked.

"Hey," she said, grabbing her juice. "I'm Madison." She looked right over at Mom. "You would not believe what happened on the field trip, Mom. "

"So tell me," Mom said.

Madison looked over at Paul and shrugged. "Maybe I'll tell you later."

Mom wrapped her arm around Madison's shoulders. "Come on, honey bear. Tell me. I'm sure Paul would love to hear your story."

"Well, I have homework," Madison mumbled.

"I'll tell you later. Nice to meet you." She nodded to Paul and walked out of the kitchen.

"Maddie!" Mom yelled after her. Phin was following, too. "Are you okay? What was all that about?"

"Nothing. Forget it," Madison said. "I'm going up to my room."

Madison grabbed her laptop from the den and headed upstairs. She didn't care about the mess. She didn't care about the hole in her ceiling. She didn't even care if Billy the contractor was up there working.

All she cared about was being in *her* space—and calling Fiona's house to see if her best friend was feeling any better since the bee incident.

Fiona's telephone line was busy the first, second, and sixth times Madison tried. Figuring that maybe Fiona was online, Madison plugged in her modem and logged on to bigfishbowl.com. Unfortunately, Fiona wasn't in any of the chat rooms, either, and when Madison checked her buddy list, she didn't find Fiona's name.

The only name Madison recognized there was Bigwheels.

So she sent her an Insta-Message.

```
<MadFinn>: hola
<Bigwheels>: do u take Spanish
<MadFinn>: Just barely. Whassup?
<Bigwheels>: N2M
<MadFinn>: well %-6
```

```
<Bigwheels>: huh????
<MadFinn>: I am totally brain-dead
    b/c I just got back fm a field
    trip and my friend needed to be
    rushed to the doctor it was like
    some reality show on TV
<Bigwheels>: wow
<MadFinn>: how r things w/Lainie
    today?
<Bigwheels>: still not so great
<MadFinn>: what happened on ur
    hiking trip
<Bigwheels>: I don't wanna talk
    about it right now
<MadFinn>: I can't be a real keypal
    unless u tell me the truth.
    Remember we said—no secrets.
<Bigwheels>: I know
<MadFinn>: so?
<Bigwheels>: GTG—school
<MadFinn>: what?
<Bigwheels>: *poof*
```

Madison couldn't believe it. She tried to Insta-Message Bigwheels a second time, but her keypal had already logged off.

Was Bigwheels writing from school and that was why she couldn't say much more?

Madison was a little worried. She opened a new e-mail and addressed it. She had some advice for her keypal after all.

From: MadFinn
To: Bigwheels
Subject: You Got Offline So Fast
Date: Fri 30 Mar 4:21 PM

I was bummed when you got off the
computer w/o telling me what was
REALLY bothering you. You don't
sound ok at all. I know this thing
w/Lainie is stinky, but it won't
last 4ever. I have friend fights 2
and they always, ALWAYS work out.
Well, mostly they do. Except for
Poison Ivy LOL.

Today's trip was a little weird 4
me 2. We were @ this nature center
and my friend Fiona got stung by
this enormous bee. It must have
been huge because her arm all
swelled up like an inflatable raft.

I think u should call Lainie right
now and ask her what's up. Maybe if
u talk 1 on 1 she will be nicer?
Maybe she has a good reason for not
telling u something. Maybe she's
embarrassed or too scared. You
should try.

I hope u write back sooner than
soon. I will be waiting.

Yours till the bees wax,

MadFinn

P.S. At the field trip, we also saw these incredibly beautiful butterflies. This is the symbol for a pretty little butterfly: {(i)}

"What are you doing up here?" Mom said. She'd been standing in the doorway to Madison's water-damaged bedroom.

"I'm online," Madison said. "Where's *Paul*?"

Mom walked over and sat on the edge of Madison's bed, even though it was covered with a plastic cover. "He left."

"Oh," Madison said.

"Is that what's bugging you? Paul?" Mom asked. "You really have a bee in your bonnet today."

Madison stared at Mom. "Why do you say *that*?"

"First of all, you come storming into the house like it's on fire. You growl at me in the kitchen. Now you're up here in the half dark working at a messy desk in a room that needs to be cleaned and repaired—"

"So?" Madison said.

"Honey bear, what is going on? You have me a little worried," Mom said. She reached over and wrapped her arms around Madison.

Madison's eyes filled up. Then her bottom lip started to quiver. Within moments, she was bawling.

"Oh, Maddie," Mom said. "What is it?"

"Fiona got stung by a bee today," Madison said. "At the nature center. And everyone was helping her, but I thought she was going to die or something—"

"Shhhhhh," Mom said. "Hush. She's fine."

"How do you know?" Madison said through her tears.

"She called a little earlier and left a message. She wanted you to know she was at home and feeling better."

Madison sighed. "She called?"

Mom reached around and wiped off some of Madison's tears with her sleeve. She touched her cheek very softly. They sat there together in silence for a few moments.

"You know, it really smells up here," Madison blurted.

"What?" Mom cried.

"It smells like wet, damp, icky room," Madison said. "Can we go downstairs now?"

She was still sniffling as they headed down to the first floor.

"I'm sorry, Mom. I'm sorry I was so mean."

Mom just smiled. "You weren't mean," she said. "You were just upset."

When they got down in the kitchen, Mom made Madison a cup of hot chocolate. It was getting past the winter and into full-time spring, so the "cocoa days" were numbered. Madison only liked drinking it when she was feeling cold or feeling blue. That usually meant only in winters—or times like right now.

Mom stood over by the kitchen sink while Madison explained everything that had happened that day on the field trip. Mom couldn't believe all the mishaps, especially the bruise on Madison's shoulder from where the Frisbee hit.

"What a day!" she said.

"Mom . . ." Madison said her name very slowly. "Who was that Paul guy?"

"Someone I know from work. A film editor, actually," Mom said. "He's very funny. Well, you didn't really get a chance to talk to him, but he is. I know you would like him."

"Are you guys dating or what?" Madison asked.

"Dating?" Mom laughed. "Don't be silly."

"Why is that such a silly question?" Madison asked.

"Maddie, if I'm going to date someone, you're going to know about it."

"Did you meet him on Date-O-Magic?" Madison snapped.

"Where?" Mom said. She sat down in the chair next to Madison's chair. "What do you know about *Date-O-Magic*?"

"I know you surf that Web site—" Madison started to say.

She cut herself off. *Whoops.* Now Mom would know she'd been nosing around the computer.

Sure enough, Mom crossed her arms and made an "Oh, you do?" face. "Have we been snooping around on my computer?" she asked.

Madison skipped right over what she'd done to get to the heart of what she wanted to say. "Mom, do you know what happens to people who date other people from online? Don't you ever watch those shows on TV? On the news once they had a story about this guy who got this woman to leave her whole family and move across the country to be with him," Madison said. "She left her *kids* behind and moved to the middle of nowhere."

Mom sighed. "Do you think that's what I'm going to do?"

"Well," Madison said.

Mom stood up from the kitchen table and poured herself a cup of hot chocolate. She sat back down and pushed closer to Madison, reaching out for her daughter's wrist, holding on to it tightly while she explained herself.

"I'm not dating anyone from the Internet, Maddie," Mom said seriously. "And I don't want you to worry that I might ever do that. I know plenty of people have met dates online. My friend Olga gave me the Web site address to check into it. But I'm not ready for all that."

"Really?" Madison asked.

Mom smiled. "Really."

Madison squeezed her mom's wrist right back.

"Maddie, I wouldn't date anyone without talking to you about it, okay?" Mom said.

"You mean like asking my permission?" Madison asked.

"Well, no," Mom said. "Not exactly. But I would want you to know who I was going with and where we were going. I would want to include you in all my major decisions."

Madison sighed. "Oh. I guess I can handle that."

"Are we okay now?" Mom said. She put their cocoa cups into the dishwasher and wiped down the countertop. Madison didn't answer right away, so Mom decided to sneakily change the subject. "Maddie, why don't you try to call Fiona back? She sounded like she really wanted to talk. I'm sure she'd love to talk to you after the day she had."

Madison jumped out of her chair for the phone. That was a very good idea. She didn't feel like talking about Mom or Mom's dates anymore.

This time when she dialed, Fiona answered.

Madison listened while Fiona rambled on for a half hour about how strange it was that she'd passed out—even for the shortest time. "I never do that!" she said. And Fiona didn't even remember when the doctor gave her the shot with the gigantic needle.

After she hung up, Madison checked online for another response from Bigwheels. But there were no keypal e-mails to be found. The only things in Madison's bigfishbowl.com mailbox were another joke from Dad and another coupon from Boop-Dee-Doop. She deleted them both and opened her files. She was typing for almost an hour when Mom came into the den with some "news." Madison wanted to scream.

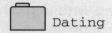 Dating

The crisis continues.

Mom and I just had this conversation like an hour ago about how she would NEVER (she said that like ten times) go out without talking to me. Now all of a sudden she gets a call from PAUL (I hate that name BTW) and comes into the den and tells me that he invited her to dinner Saturday. So now she is going on a date tomorrow! TWO days!!! Even worse, she called my dad right away to ask him to take me to dinner that night and watch me until she comes back. How weird is THAT?

This week everyone is bugging me: contractors like Billy, all boys (esp. Egg and Hart), teachers like Mr. Danehy, who act like they know everything, Ivy (of course), Aimee when she gets hysterical, Dad, who won't cook for me anymore, my keypal who won't tell me her real problems, and now even Mom and her date-to-be, Paul.

Sometimes junior high stinks in a big way.

It's like a stink-BUG. LOL.

Rude Awakening: I wish I had a giant flyswatter for seventh grade. That way I could take care of all the pests with one big SPLAT.

Chapter 11

Madison didn't get any new e-mail from Bigwheels the next day. She could think of nothing except Mom's dinner with Paul. Mom had saved that date just for him, even marking it on the refrigerator calendar in red ink. That was serious. She marked most things in pencil.

Despite her anxieties, however, Madison was happy to watch Mom get ready for the big Saturday night date. It felt like forever since she'd seen Mom get dressed up for *anything*. Madison watched Mom curl her hair at the ends and apply a rosy blush.

"Do you think I should wear Suddenly Red or Plum Perfection with this dress?" Mom asked Madison excitedly, holding up two lipstick tubes.

"Are you planning on kissing this guy, Mom? On the first date?" Madison said with a frown.

"Listen to me," Mom said. "I sound like I'm in—"

"Junior high!" Madison said, finishing Mom's sentence.

Mom smiled. "Oh, honey bear. Be nice. I never go out like this anymore."

Madison apologized.

"Well, you look very pretty," Madison told her mom. "And this Paul guy's going to be happy when he gets here. Trust me."

"I feel like getting spiffy tonight," Mom said.

Madison wrinkled up her nose. "What's spiffy? Sounds like floor cleaner."

"Getting all dressed up. I haven't gone on a date in so long, I don't know what to wear, what to say," Mom confided. "I want this to be perfect."

"Nothing is perfect, Mom," Madison said. "You always say that to me."

"I know," she said, leaning over to give Madison a kiss. "Except you."

"Oh, Mom, not now!"

Mom laughed and slipped on her gray stockings and sling-back pumps.

"So give it to me straight," she said, posing with her arms outstretched. "Good or bad?"

Madison just applauded.

Minutes later, the phone rang. Dad was "running late" but "on his way."

As she reapplied her mascara, Mom looked over

at Madison. "At least your father is consistent," she said.

When the doorbell zinged, Madison opened the front door with a dramatic "Hey, Dad!"

"These are for my dinner date," he said in a goofy voice, bending down like some kind of prince. He presented Madison with a small bouquet of daisies.

"For me?" Madison said coyly. She giggled.

"You look delightful this evening, young lady," Dad said, continuing to act all mushy. Madison liked it, even though she knew there was nothing particularly delightful about her blue jeans and T-shirt.

"Is Stephanie waiting in the car?" Madison asked.

Dad shook his head. "Nope. Just you and me, kid, for a night on the town."

That news made Madison smile even wider. She hadn't been on a dinner *alone* with Dad in ages. Stephanie had practically moved into Dad's apartment over the last month, so Madison was just beginning to settle on the idea that she might never again have an "alone" dinner with Dad.

Until now.

"I thought we'd hit Casey's Burger Stop and then head on over to the Bowl-a-Lot lanes. Sounds like fun, right?" Dad said.

"Rowrrooooo!" Phinnie appeared from the

other room, tail wagging. He pounced on Dad.

"Hey, pugster!" Dad cried. Madison chuckled to herself when he said that because it sounded so much like "Finnster."

Her mind wandered to thoughts of Hart Jones. Despite this week's not-so-hot field trip and Hart's lamer-than-lame behavior in science class, Madison still got mini-heart palpitations at the mere *idea* of him. What would she do if she ever went on a real date with Hart someday?

"Is your mother upstairs?" Dad asked, interrupting Madison's silent reverie. "I need to talk to her for just a sec."

The total plan for the night was for Dad to take Madison to dinner and then "watch over" her (Madison couldn't deal with the term *baby-sit* since she was twelve going on thirteen). They'd stay at the Blueberry Street house until Mom came home from her own date.

"Frannie?" Dad called up the stairs. He stopped at the bottom, looking up with a gaze of disbelief as Mom descended in her beautiful dress and sling-back heels.

"Jeff! You're here," Mom said, sounding a bit surprised and relieved all at the same time. Luckily Dad had arrived in time to avoid an uncomfortable confrontation between him and Mom's new date, Paul, who was due to arrive fifteen minutes from now.

117

"Frannie," Dad continued, his jaw slackening. "You look . . . you look . . . absolutely stunning."

Madison couldn't believe Dad sounded tongue-tied. And she hadn't seen him stare at Mom that way in a long time.

"Thank you, Jeff," Mom said. "That's very kind."

Mom puckered and smiled. Madison noticed that she'd picked the Plum Perfection lip color. It did indeed look like *perfection*. She strolled gingerly across the living room, smelling of lilacs, the perfume she wore only for very special occasions. Phinnie followed. He must have liked the smell.

From what Madison could tell, Dad liked the smell, too. He still had a faraway look in his eye. He couldn't take his eyes off Mom.

"So you two have something fun planned tonight?" Mom asked, breaking the silence.

"We're going for burgers and bowling," Madison announced.

Dad jumped right in. "Yeah, Bowl-a-Lot lanes. You know that place."

"Great," Mom said, not looking at Dad, glancing out the front window. "Well, I don't want to keep you two from your exciting plans. . . ."

With that one nonglance, Dad got the hint.

Time to go.

"So the plan is for me to bring Maddie back here after our dinner. We'll hang out until you get home," Dad said. "Sound good?"

Mom nodded.

Madison nodded.

She leaned over to kiss Mom good-bye. "Have a nice date, Mom," she whispered.

Dad took Mom's hand and told her again how pretty she looked. It seemed like he didn't want to let go.

"Thanks again, Jeff," Mom said again, gently tugging free from his grip. "See ya soon, honey bear." She waved to Madison.

Madison raced Dad out to the car. For the first time in a very long time, she'd be riding shotgun, and that was *all* that mattered right now. She buckled up her seat belt, and they sped away to dinner.

The burger place was jam-packed with families waiting for tables when they arrived, so Madison and Dad sat at the counter instead. Dad hated waiting. They ordered well-done burgers and milk shakes that were served right away. It wasn't as great as eating a homemade meal in Dad's apartment, but it was definitely an adventure.

Madison told Dad about her other adventures of the week, too: the nature center field trip, Fiona's bee sting, the upcoming megaproject on Amelia Earhart, and everything in between.

"Gee, you sure are busy," Dad said. "Maybe Mom was right. You have an awful lot going on between school and volunteering, don't you think? Too much?"

"How much is too much?" Madison asked.

"Did you have a chance to download that Calendar Girl software?" he asked. Madison said she'd show him the program when they got back to the house.

Dad slurped the last of his milk shake. He seemed strangely distracted.

"Your mother looked so nice tonight," he said. "Who's she going on a date with?"

"How should I know?" Madison said. "His name is Paul, I think."

"Not Paul Pierce from Budge Films," Dad said.

"Who's that?" Madison replied. "Yeah, I think Mom said she works with the guy. I can't remember."

"Hmmph," Dad muttered to himself. "I always thought he had a thing for your mother."

"Huh?" Madison said. "Daddy, what are you talk-ing about?"

"Oh." Dad caught his breath. "Nothing. I was just thinking out loud. Sorry."

"Can we go bowling now?" she asked.

"Let me just pay the check," Dad said, getting up from their table.

Madison popped her last french fry into her mouth.

As usual, the Bowl-a-Lot bowling shoes didn't fit right. Madison's little toes always felt supersquished inside them. She wore a size five, but lately her feet seemed to be growing very quickly. She asked for a pair in size six. It was just one more body change she'd have to get used to.

Madison and Dad were assigned to lane 13, which she immediately considered unlucky, being the superstitious seventh grader that she was. She scanned the rows of lanes to see if there was another one free so they could trade. But all the other lanes were full.

While glancing around the Bowl-a-Lot lobby, Madison thought she heard a familiar voice. It was coming from the middle of a crowd over by the refreshment stand. Just as Madison realized whose voice it was, she saw her.

Poison Ivy Daly.

Ivy was with her sister, carrying a tray of nachos and heading back toward their own bowling lane, number 4. They were at Bowl-a-Lot with their dad, too. Madison believed in coincidences, but she couldn't explain how she and Ivy would be traveling in the same orbit tonight. She shrugged that off, too, happy that Ivy hadn't seen her and happier than happy that their bowling lane was miles away from the Dalys'.

"Prepare to lose," Dad joked as he wrote their names onto the scoring sheet. An overhead projection with special effects welcomed them to their lane. Dad was joking, of course, but nonetheless, he loved competition. As soon as he hit the start button, a message popped up onto the screen: "Get ready to bowl, Madison!" He yelled out the words.

Maddie tried to act as if he hadn't just screeched her name for the entire establishment to hear and walked over to pick out her own bowling ball. She found the smallest, lightest ball there, a sparkle-orange one with small holes for her fingers. Madison bent down and dropped the ball between her legs, watching as it rolled slowly down lane 13.

"We're going to be here all night!" Dad yelled. He liked to tease Madison about the way she threw the ball. He expected her to run up and whip it down the alley, but Madison was too afraid her fingers would get stuck and she'd fly down toward the pins with the ball.

Her first ball knocked over three pins, which wasn't so hot. Unfortunately, her next attempt was a gutter ball.

Dad told her not to worry and hopped up to grab a giant bowling ball for himself. He wound up his arms like he was doing some kind of chicken dance and did a few deep-knee bends. Then he launched his ball down lane 13.

Strike!

He cackled, clapping, when the pins fell. A few people next to them looked over at all the commotion, which embarrassed Madison a teeny bit. She casually glanced down toward lane 4 to make certain that Ivy Daly hadn't heard any of Dad's noisy display.

"Hot diggety!" he said, smacking his knee. He was getting more embarrassing by the moment.

"Dad?" Madison said softly. "Can you keep it down just a little? You're so loud."

He smiled. "Sure, honey," he said, patting her shoulder. "Sure! Now it's your turn. Go get 'em!" Despite what he'd just said, Dad started clapping and cheering *again*.

Madison noticed the woman in the next lane— *staring*.

It was one thing to suspect someone was over-hearing Dad's antics, but when that fact was con-firmed, Madison wanted to run—far away.

"Go, Maddie, go!" Dad clapped again.

She threw two more gutter balls.

By the time the first game was completed, Madison's bowling score was twenty-one. Dad had scored almost a hundred, just missing another strike in the last frame.

"Can we go?" Madison asked once he'd tab-ulated the scores.

"Already?" Dad said. He sounded disappointed. "I thought we'd stay for at least two games. I like being out on a father-daughter date with you!"

Madison glanced down the alley to see if anyone had heard him say that. Were Ivy and her family still playing? They were. Madison believed this was her one chance to escape without being seen by the enemy—and without getting more embarrassed. The grandmother in the next lane was eyeing them again.

Madison avoided her glance at all costs.

"I'm tired," she lied to Dad. "And we should get back to walk Phinnie."

They took off their bowling shoes and went back out to the car. Madison hustled along faster than usual just in case Ivy happened to glance back and see her there. She couldn't see *anyone* she knew. This date was like one big gutter ball as far as Madison was concerned.

Run.

She wondered if Mom's date was turning out any better.

When they pulled into the driveway back home and climbed the stoop, Madison heard Phin wailing. Dad offered to take him for a quick walk while Madison went inside. Dog and Dad were only gone for a minute.

"Hey, Maddie," Dad said. "What do you call a cat who knows how to bowl?"

Madison groaned. "Oh, Dad." She prepared herself for the punch line.

"An alley cat." Dad chuckled to himself as he took off Phin's leash.

Madison went into the other room and clicked on the television.

Lame-o.

"Let's have some hot chocolate or something," Dad suggested. He followed Madison into the den. "Hey, wait a minute, are you *still* sleeping down here?" he asked.

"Mom says the contractor is coming back to replace the roof shingles," Madison said, clicking the channels without stopping. "And then I can go back into my room. Finally."

Dad sat down on the sofa and wrapped his arm around Madison. "I wish your mother would just let me help her with repairs like that once in a while," he said.

Me too, Madison thought. She leaned into Dad's side, and they watched TV together.

Madison assumed they must have fallen fast asleep, because the next thing she remembered was the sound of Mom's voice. Mom was standing directly over Madison and Dad with a smirk on her face.

"Wake up, you two," she whispered. "I'm home."

Madison blinked. Phin jumped off the sofa. Dad shook off his sleep, waving his arms and jumping up.

"Whooooee," Dad said. "Some guardian I make! Falling asleep on the job. Sorry 'bout that, Frannie."

"You two looked sweet," Mom said, smiling. "I can't thank you enough for coming, Jeff."

Madison looked at her mom's face—glowing. Her cheeks looked pink, like she'd been sunburned with happiness. Neither Madison nor Dad had seen that look in a long, long time.

Dad leaned over to give Madison a kiss good-bye. As he walked away, Madison felt her chest contract, like she'd just swallowed an ice cube or a big wad of gum. Something was stuck in her throat: a funny feeling, a weird sensation, and the realization that Mom and Dad were *never* getting back together.

"I am SO exhausted!" Mom said after he'd gone. She was still glowing from her date. "Bedtime for me."

"You're not even going to tell me about your date?" Madison said. She pulled Mom's arm to come sit on the sofa, but Mom resisted.

"I really do have to get to bed now," she said softly. She brushed the hair out of Madison's eye. "You had a nice time on your date with Dad, though?"

Madison shrugged. "So-so. Bowling really stinks."

"But I thought you liked it," Mom said.

"What about *your* date, Mom?" Madison pleaded. "You haven't even given me a little clue about your date."

Mom laughed. "We got along very well," she said.

Madison raised an eyebrow. "And?"

"Oh, Maddie, and I'll tell you everything else tomorrow," Mom said, walking away. "I promise." She blew a kiss.

As soon as Mom left the den, Madison booted up her laptop computer and went into her files.

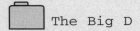 The Big D

Rude Awakening: Better date than never.

I used to think that I couldn't deal with Dad dating. But I got used to Stephanie. I even like her a lot now.

And just this week I thought the world would go to pieces if Mom went out with some stranger. But now she went. And she looks happy. Really and truly, she looks like someone put on a flashlight behind her eyes. Even Dad saw.

I can't believe I'm saying this, but I'm glad Mom went on a date. I'm glad that she's starting to feel pretty again.

I just wish I could I could figure out the boys in my life, too. Like I'll probably be date-phobic with Hart forever. Not that he'd ever ask me out, of course.

Bigwheels would probably tell me that I have nothing to worry about. But I can't help it!

Madison hit SAVE and turned off her computer. She was looking forward to tomorrow. Her mind buzzed with different questions. Would Ivy be nice in science class for the presentation? Why hadn't Bigwheels written again?

After an overdose of parents, Madison needed a superdose of friends.

Girl friends.

Chapter 12

Madison finished her Amelia Earhart paper Saturday while Billy worked on repairing the wet ceiling in her bedroom. Thanks to his roof and chimney repairs, there were no more surprise leaks. She'd have her own room back like new very soon. Mom was busy working, too. Madison heard her talking on the phone to Paul more than once.

Sunday afternoon Madison and her friends spent some time together, but not as much as she wanted. Since Fiona was still a little nauseated after the bee sting, Madison went over to her house and hand-delivered the butterfly puzzle she'd purchased at the nature center. Fiona loved it.

By the time Monday morning rolled around, Madison was ready for things to get back to normal, whatever that was. Aimee and Fiona were ready, too.

"They gave me this cream to keep the swelling down," Fiona explained to Madison and Aimee before classes that morning. "And I've been using it all weekend, but I still look puffy. I miss the old, nonpuffy me."

"Your eyes are still kind of swollen, but everything else looks okay," Aimee said, leaning in for a closer look. "I see little red spots, but not as many as the other day."

"I think you look GREAT," Madison said, trying to be encouraging. She pulled Aimee backward and elbowed her in the side. "Don't you think she looks mostly *good*, Aimee?"

"Yeah, I guess now you do," Aimee said. "I thought you were going to go into a coma or something right on the field trip. I mean, can you imagine? What would they have done?"

"Aimee!" Madison said.

Fiona giggled. "Thanks for your encouragement, Aim. And I do feel fine. Except for the puffy eyes, the itching, and this," she said. She produced an inhaler and held it up for a hallway show-and-tell.

Egg and Drew rushed over to where they were standing. The girls immediately crossed their arms, like they were waiting for the boys to go away.

"Hey, Fiona," Egg said, not going anywhere. "How are you feeling? Chet said you're on all this medicine. Are you feeling better? I hope so."

Aimee snickered a little at all of his attention, but Fiona smiled sweetly. "Thanks, Egg. I'm feeling fine."

"How are you guys doing?" Drew asked Madison and Aimee.

Aimee just rolled her eyes.

"If you need help with that math assignment, Fiona, call me." Egg grabbed Drew's sleeve and headed back down the hall. "See you later, okay?"

Aimee's mouth was flapping open. "OH MY GOD! What was THAT?" She let out a huge laugh.

"What?" Fiona said, still scratching her arms. "Why are you looking at me like that? Stop laughing. And please don't say anything about—"

"Did you give Egg some kind of nice potion or what? He's being so sweet, it's enough to make me gag." Aimee covered her mouth in another overdramatic pose. "You sure you've been telling us *everything* about you and Egg?"

Madison opened her locker and grabbed books for English class. "Yeah, Fiona," she said. "You guys aren't going out or anything, are you?"

No one had ever really asked Fiona point-blank if she and Egg were dating. Had they ever held hands? Had they ever *kissed*?

Brrrrring.

"See you after science," Fiona said to Madison, heading in the opposite direction. She escaped without answering the most important question.

Aimee chased after Fiona down the hall. "Yeah, see you, Maddie!"

Madison slammed her locker shut.

"FINNSTER!" Hart blurted. He was standing right there behind the locker door. "Going to science?"

"Where did you come from?" Madison asked, a little startled.

"I was down the hall. But I'm going to science, too," he said. He rotated his neck to the side, and his tousled brown hair fell softly over his forehead. Madison felt an urge to move it away with her hand but was grateful that she didn't do anything embarrassing like that. He would be *completely* surprised if she touched his head. And what if someone saw?

What was she thinking?

Chet came rushing over. He broke Madison's train of thought.

"Hey, man, I was looking for you down the hall," Chet said to Hart. "Where did you go?"

Madison stared at the floor, and the three walked down the corridor together. Once again she had lost her ability to speak in front of Hart, a momentary condition that struck her in the strangest places. The only good thing about its happening right now was the fact that Chet took up the lull in conversation. With two guy friends nattering on and on in their own personal code language, Madison didn't really even have to speak.

Mr. Danehy was on time. And the trio barely made it to their seats before the second bell rang— and he slammed the door.

"Now!" he announced with great authority.

The whole class hushed.

"That's better," Mr. Danehy continued. "Now, preceding our bee scare last week, the science-center trip appeared to be going very well. Would you agree?"

No one said a word.

"Hello?" Mr. Danehy asked again. "Is everyone awake out there?"

"That trip was mad fun," Chet said, looking around to his other guy friends for corroboration of how he saw the trip.

Ivy just sat there, twirling one of her loop earrings. "And we learned things," she said. She looked over at Madison.

"*Lots* of things," Madison said, without thinking.

Mr. Danehy appeared impressed.

"So when we started our little field-trip experiment, I assigned you into groups of girls versus boys. I noticed a little anxiety about this while we were out in the field. Is this still true?"

"No way!" a boy in the front of the class yelled.

"So we should continue to have presentations with boys versus girls tomorrow?" Mr. Danehy asked as if he were holding a democratic vote.

Everyone agreed.

Ivy leaned over to Madison again. In light of the classroom competition, she didn't look like an enemy today. She was an ally—an ally against an even greater enemy: BOYS.

After science, Madison was so preoccupied with

the upcoming showdown that she almost forgot her after-school trip to Mrs. Wing's computer laboratory. She'd promised to help out again with the school Web site, even if it also meant dealing with Egg and Drew.

Busy as a bee.

Drew brought his digital camera to Mrs. Wing's lab. He had taken dozens of photos at the seventh-grade field trip. Madison looked through them, laughing. She wrote captions for the photos he printed out and put into a pile called MAYBE. The pile next to that was REJECTS.

Madison laughed hardest when she came to a photograph of Ranger Lester looking official in his safari gear. He was leaning on a tree.

She marked that caption THE RANGER GETS LOST IN THE FOREST. Mrs. Wing made her change it later on to MEET RANGER LESTER.

There were candid photos, too, of classmates. Drew had snapped one picture on the bus ride over to the field trip. As it would happen, it was a shot of Madison and Ivy. They almost looked like friends in the photo.

"Hey," Drew said. "We should put that one up."

"Very funny, Drewfus," Madison said. She used a silly nickname Chet always used. Drew didn't like it one bit.

Drew ignored her and showed Madison more photos: a chrysalis in the butterfly sanctuary, Jimmy the field guide (looking as cute as ever), a group of boys standing around while the doctor dealt with Fiona's bee sting. He had lots of photographs of the stinging incident. It had been the highlight of the trip, after all.

After helping write more captions, Madison, Drew, and Mrs. Wing downloaded a whole new Field Trip page onto the school site.

"You both did a fabulous job," Mrs. Wing said. She waved her arms into the air with a "Hoorah," and her charm bracelet jangled. Madison noticed littler-than-little charms of computers and computer mice on the bracelet. It was the ultimate accessory for a computer teacher. Madison smiled. She had one just like it.

After leaving Drew in the computer lab, Madison headed back to her locker to grab her stuff. It was almost four o'clock. She looked around for Aimee and Fiona, but they were still doing after-school dance and soccer, as usual. Madison decided to hang out and wait for them, at least for a little while.

She strolled down the hall. A few stragglers were at lockers, retrieving books and bags. School was so quiet at this time of the afternoon. Madison could hear everything.

Choral practice.

A geography-club meeting.

Teachers in the teachers' lounge.

As she headed around one corner, Madison heard

two boys talking. She recognized the voices: Hart and Chet. They were talking about science class.

She was tempted to pounce on them the way Phinnie might—take the enemy by surprise—but instead she lingered at the corner and eavesdropped on their conversation. It was hard to hear everything, but Madison was able to make out the basics of what they were saying.

Madison couldn't believe her ears.

At home that night, she couldn't wait to go online.

From: MadFinn
To: BalletGrl, Wetwinz
Subject: YOU WON'T BELIEVE THIS
Date: Mon 2 April 5:34 PM
I missed u guys at school. Waited for like a half hour but u weren't back from soccer or wherever. Where were u?

N e way, I heard Chet and Hart talking in the hallway today and I have to tell you what they said.
1. Egg likes you, Fiona. I mean, I know you know that, but those guys were making fun of him for it. Isn't that crazy? Are you glad? I don't think it's so weird anymore.

2. They think that they know everything there is to know about that science trip. But they DON'T! I heard them say that they didn't go see the duck pond part of the trip. That means we can totally beat them at our presentation. Isn't that cool?
3. Hart Jones is SOOOOOO full of himself. I actually heard him say that some girl in our class really, really likes him. Who do you think it is?

Madison stopped typing.

When she reread number 3, she realized something she hadn't thought of before. She'd originally heard him and thought it must be some other girl. But what if *she* was the one he was talking about? Did he know how she really felt?

Madison deleted number 3. She was about to sign off and send the e-mail when she realized something else she hadn't thought of before.

Why would Aimee or Fiona care about her science class?

Most of what she was sending in this e-mail was for the wrong people. Aimee and Fiona weren't in her science class. Madison needed to send the secret information about Chet to a girl who would understand *exactly* what she was feeling right now.

Only Ivy Daly fit that description. Ivy and her drones, anyway.

She rewrote and readdressed the e-mail to Ivy, which was odder than odd since she'd never, *ever* sent her enemy a personal e-mail message. Of course, Madison left out the e-mail parts about Hart (what if *Ivy* was the mystery girl?) and Egg (Ivy would just use that information as an excuse to make fun of Fiona).

She changed the address.

```
To: Flowr99
```

Less than a minute after she had hit SEND, Madison's computer bleeped.

Someone had sent her mail.

It was from Fiona! But something about the note looked suspicious. Madison wasn't sure what at first.

```
From: Wetwins
To: MadFinn
Subject: Science Notes
Date: Mon 2 April 6:00 PM
```
Hi there! Do you have notes from scienc trip. It turns
out my teacher wants us to do a papr on it. Can I borow yours please? I need info on the duck pond.

First, Madison noticed all the misspellings. Fiona never made mistakes like that. She was a good speller.

Madison paid a little closer attention to the e-mail sender's name. It wasn't from Fiona, whose screen name was Wetwinz! It was from Chet! His screen name had the *s* on the end.

Madison read it over and sighed. How could he think she wouldn't notice? He was trying to get information so the boys wouldn't lose the science challenge. Madison couldn't believe it.

Ping, ping.

Someone was sending Madison an Insta-Message.

```
<Flowr99>: hi
<MadFinn>: hi
<Flowr99>: got ur email & those
    guys r total creeps
<MadFinn>: I know
<Flowr99>: I can't believe u heard
    them say that
```

Madison wasn't sure she liked discovering how much she and Ivy seemed to have in common over the past few days.

```
<MadFinn>: so what should we do?
<Flowr99>: lemme think
```

\<MadFinn\>: we could just tell Mr. D
that they didn't go to the duck
pond

\<Flowr99\>: nah too e-z & I don't
wanna be a rat

\<MadFinn\>: we could ask them
lots of questions about the
duck pond during their
presentation

\<Flowr99\>: wait that's good

\<MadFinn\>: ask them questions?

\<Flowr99\>: NO! we can make up some
fake story and tell it to them
like we're helping them out and
then that's what they'll say at
the presentation and they will be
WRONG and they'll get a bad grade
or something

\<MadFinn\>: GIWIST

\<Flowr99\>: so let's think of
really stupid things so THEY'LL
look stupid

\<MadFinn\>: we could say someone fell
in the water

\<Flowr99\>: that's dumb what about
alligators

\<MadFinn\>: don't forget the duck
poop

\<Flowr99\>: I wanna forget THAT
thanks very much

\<MadFinn\>: what else?

```
<Flowr99>: what about piranhas
<MadFinn>: in a DUCK pond? No one
    would fall for that
<Flowr99>: they would!!! VVF look I
    gotta go
<MadFinn>: bye
<Flowr99>: *poof*
```

Ivy's sneaky side had shown itself, and Madison was basking in its sneakiness. She was readier than ready to make up a doozy of a story and convince Hart, Chet, and the others that it had really happened. Once they retold that story in front of Mr. Danehy, he would laugh them right out of the presentation—leaving the girls as winners.

The only question remaining was: How would she get the boys in Mr. Danehy's class to believe such a story?

Chapter 13

"How did I get so many e-mails in five minutes? This is crazy!" Madison told herself. She looked down at Phinnie, napping on the floor, as if he'd have the magic answer.

He just snored.

There hadn't been any messages in the mailbox when Madison had checked there ten minutes before. She figured the Web server must have been saving all the messages up to deliver them at the same time. She was busy these days, but her e-mailbox was even busier. This proved it.

FROM	SUBJECT
✉ Flowr99	Re: YOU WON'T BELIEVE THIS
✉ JeffFinn	Bowling Queen
✉ Bigwheels	The Story

She wanted to save Bigwheels's long e-mail for last so she could give it her undivided attention. Then Madison read the rest.

Ivy sent back a shorter-than-short message.

```
From: Flowr99
To: MadFinn
Subject: Re: YOU WON'T BELIEVE THIS
Date: Mon 2 April 6:15 PM
Tell me what you decide to write
Chet at lunch tomorrow. Those boys
are goners.
```

Madison smiled with glee at the idea of their plan.

But then she wondered what Aimee and Fiona would say if they knew Madison was e-mailing and planning secret rendezvous with Poison Ivy. She knew the moment the boys-versus-girls experiment was over, things would go right back to normal with Ivy, which meant no speaking except to say, "Hey, you, get out of my way," or something like that.

But now, all rules had changed—at least for one more science class.

Madison clicked onto her next e-mail, from Dad. He had left a message explaining how much he loved dinner and bowling and falling asleep with Phinnie. He called Madison "the Bowling Queen of the Galaxy."

Madison e-mailed back with a short message, too:

From: MadFinn
To: JeffFinn
Subject: Re: Bowling Queen
Date: Mon 2 April 6:30 PM
Love you Dad. I know how you feel.
I miss you at home, too, especially
when the roof leaks.

Madison scrolled down to the latest e-mail from Bigwheels.
It was a long one.

From: Bigwheels
To: MadFinn
Subject: The Whole Story
Date: Mon 2 April 6:30 PM
I know it has been a really long
time since I wrote, and I am sorry.
And I also know I have been feeling
down in the dumps.

Thanks for the {(i)}. I don't think
you know this, but butterflies are
my favorite creatures. I have a
poster on the wall in my bedroom
with an alphabet on butterfly wings.

So here is what REALLY happened

with Lainie last week. After a week
of her ignoring me at lunch and us
fighting in the halls at school and
generally not agreeing on anything,
we finally sat down to talk.
Actually, we were on a bus trip
home Friday. I think she did that
because on the bus I was stuck and
had nowhere to go if she said
something that bothered me. But it
didn't turn out so bad.

Lainie told me that she thought I
was the one who was different.
Those were her exact words. Can you
believe she said that? She thought
I was the one who seemed distant,
and that upset her, so she really
was hanging with those other girls
because she was so sad that maybe
I didn't want to be friends
anymore.

Now, Lainie and I have been bestest
friends since kindergarten. How
could I not know she was so upset?

We promised—that everything we
think and feel should be said out
loud. Just like us keypals. So
there are NO secrets ever.

And now, writing to you, I feel the same. Did I ever tell you that my real name is Victoria? I know we're not supposed to say our real names online and everything, but I want to know your first name, too. Is that okay? I am guessing maybe it's Madeline, but I don't know. Tell me if you can. But I understand if your mom doesn't want you to tell.

So here I am at the beginning of the week and Lainie and I are real friends again. And you are a real friend, too. I wish you lived near me. We could ALL be pals.

Yours till the duck quacks,

Victoria

(aka Bigwheels)

P.S. Good luck in ur science presentation tomorrow.

Madison took a deep breath. She was so relieved that Bigwheels and Lainie had made up. After all the worrying and all the misunderstandings, everything worked out.

Even more exciting, Madison now knew Bigwheels's *real* name.

"Excuse me!" Mom called out from the doorway to the den. She looked at her watch as if to say, "Do you know how late it is?"

Madison stopped midthought and closed her laptop as if she'd shut it down. Of course, she didn't turn it off. Not yet.

"Have you been on the computer all this time?" Mom asked, talking over herself. "Don't you have some homework to do?"

Mom was right, as usual. Madison had math problems to finish. Madison got up off the den sofa and pulled her orange bag to over by the computer.

"And no television while you study, either," Mom said. "I want lights out tonight at a reasonable hour. You spend too much time typing away on that computer, Maddie."

Madison frowned. "But I love it, Mom," she said.

"Well, I don't like it when you're always so busy, busy, busy," Mom said.

"Look at *you*!" Madison blurted. "You're always working."

"That isn't true," Mom said.

"And you haven't even told me about your date with that Paul guy."

Mom scratched her head. "Not much to tell."

"Where did you go?" Madison asked.

"French restaurant," Mom replied. "And then we went for a walk."

"A walk?" Madison asked. "What for?"

Mom just grinned.

"No way!" Madison squealed. She thought about movies where people walked hand in hand into dark, undiscovered spots. There they'd lock lips.

And Mom was wearing Plum Perfection. . . .

"You have some imagination, honey bear," Mom said. "We just went for a walk—and talked."

"What did you talk about?" Madison asked.

"Work, mostly," Mom said. She thought about Madison's earlier comment. "Maybe you're right. I do work all the time, even when I'm not *at* work."

"So are you going out again? Did he ask you again?" Madison asked.

Mom shook her head. "He said he'd call me."

"Is that good or bad?" Madison asked.

"I think we'll go out again, if that's what you're asking me. He said something about grabbing a cup of coffee tomorrow."

"TOMORROW?" Madison said. Phinnie must have heard her, because he leaped onto the sofa with a burst of excitement. "That's so soon."

"I know." Mom smiled. "Tomorrow is a big day, I guess."

As Mom walked out of the room to leave Madison alone with her math problems and her laptop, the words really sank in.

Tomorrow is a big day.

She opened the computer again and proceeded with the plan A that she and Ivy devised. Madison went back to Chet's original "fake" e-mail and clicked REPLY. Then she whipped up a fantastic, exaggerated, funny e-Mail in response. Not only did she embellish the duck-pond story, but Madison invented another important tale, too, just for fun. She was practically giggling by the time she hit SEND.

Would Chet fall for it or not?

```
From: MadFinn
To: Wetwins
Subject: Re: Science Notes
Date: Mon 2 April 6:57 PM
```
Fiona—I'm sending along a page from my science notes. I hope it's the one you needed. It tells everything we saw and heard at the duck pond.

Also wanted to tell you something else I heard. Major gossip. I heard that Joan Kenyon in our class has the HUGEST crush on your brother, Chet. She was saying that she'd give anything if he would just talk to her more in school. I wonder if he will.

Bye! Maddie

148

Madison wished she could see the look on Chet and Hart's faces when they read notes about alligators and piranhas. She was ashamed to admit how much fun she was having through all the conspiring—with the enemy and without. Their science class showdown had finally arrived, and she was readier than ready.

Madison had been saving *this* date for a super-payback.

And it was finally here.

Chapter 14

"Are we ready to make our presentations now?" Mr. Danehy asked.

Madison squirmed in her chair.

The moment of truth.

Ivy scribbled a note in the margin of her notebook and shoved it onto Madison's desk.

This is gonna be fun. Did you see Hart looking over here? I am psyched to see what they do.

Chet and Hart, ever confident, volunteered to go first with their presentation. Two other boys joined them. Madison recognized them as the boys who'd whipped the Frisbee at her shoulder.

Everything about the boys' presentation went very well at first. Mr. Danehy went over all the questions from the list on the sheet he'd passed out. Hart answered everything correctly. Chet made jokes. Everyone was laughing.

Then they reached the part of the presentation about the duck pond.

"So, what did you see at the pond?" Mr. Danehy asked.

Chet grinned a giant grin. He looked over to Hart and nodded.

"Well," Hart started to explain. "I know it's weird, but there was a big fish tank set up near the pond."

"Oh, really?" Mr. Danehy said, perking up.

A girl in the back row started to say, "Hey, Mr. Danehy, there was NO—" but Ivy coughed and cut her off.

"Well," Hart continued, glancing around the room. "It's totally true. Ranger Lester showed us this special fish tank that was set up near the pond. And they keep these fish in there. . . ."

"Yes, well, what *kind* of fish?" Mr. Danehy asked.

"Um . . . piranhas?" Hart replied.

Ivy stifled a giggle.

Hart looked over in her direction and cleared his throat. "That's what it said."

"Um . . . didn't you see the tank, Mr. Danehy?" Chet interrupted. "I saw it, I swear."

"Well, you can swear all you want, Chet, but I do not remember seeing any flesh-eating fish at the

151

nature preserve," Mr. Danehy said. "I certainly hope that the girls have recorded their observations a little more carefully." He asked Hart, Chet, and the other presenters to sit back down again.

"Excuse me." Chet raised his hand and spoke up again. "Is there a problem with *our* observations?" He nervously glanced over at Madison.

He knew.

In the battle of girls versus boys, victory was now clear. The girls had duped the boys, fair and square. Chet was seething.

Now it was time for Madison, Ivy, the drones, and a few other girls to present their answers to the questions. But when it came to sharing what they had seen at the duck pond, the girls were very clear: ducks, ducks, and more ducks. *That was it.*

Mr. Danehy, who rarely smiled, cracked a sliver of a grin when they finished speaking.

"Well, girls, that's more like it. I definitely do remember lots of ducks at the duck pond," Mr. Danehy said. "Makes sense. Doesn't it, boys?"

"And duck poop, of course," Madison joked.

The boys weren't laughing, but Mr. Danehy was. The rest of the girls laughed, too. Ivy even gave Madison a high five, which took Madison by surprise. They hadn't bonded over anything since third grade, and here they were clapping hands in the middle of class.

Madison knew there was something strange

152

about connecting with Ivy now. She wasn't sure she liked playing tricks on the boys. Not like this. Was it *really* worth it to conspire and make Hart and Chet look silly in front of everyone? Was it really worth embarrassing her friends?

"That was classic," Ivy cackled. "I love watching people look dumb."

"I—I guess . . ." Madison stammered.

Mr. Danehy pronounced the girls winners in the science-class challenge. They were excused from homework and quizzes for a week.

"Now, that's a gyp," Ivy whispered to Madison. "We deserve more than that for what we did."

"I—I guess . . ." Madison said again as they left the classroom.

On the way out, a girl from the back row passed by and whispered to Madison and Ivy, "That wasn't very nice, you know." She had her nose up in the air.

"Whatever," Ivy said, rolling her eyes. "Who cares what you think?"

Madison turned her eyes to the floor.

Hart came out with Chet and some other guys, but they walked right past her and Ivy and headed into the hall.

For the first time in a week, Madison was sad to see her crush walk in the opposite direction. She wanted to hear a friendly, "Hey, Finnster!" She wanted to stand right next to him the way she had at the nature center.

"I have to go," Ivy said all of a sudden. "Later."

Madison walked off in the opposite direction to meet up with Aimee and Fiona. They'd want a full report on who had won the science competition.

"SO?" they said in unison when Madison found them.

"Girls won," Madison said, a little dejectedly.

"Cool!" Fiona said. "Chet is going to be soooo mad."

"You can say that again," Madison said. "More than you know."

"Not like I have a problem with him getting mad," Fiona joked.

Madison wanted to smile, but she didn't feel up to it.

"I have to go," Aimee said. "I have a dance lesson. Are you ready to walk home?"

As the three BFFs passed through the main part of the school yard, Madison glanced at every group of guys she saw, hoping to catch a glimpse of Hart. She wanted to apologize. But the only boys she saw were Egg and Drew, sitting over by one of the benches, talking to Dan Ginsburg.

No Hart.

Ivy Daly and her drones were standing on the other side by the parking lot, waiting for someone's mom or dad to pick them up. Madison raised her arm to wave, but Ivy didn't look over.

"Who are you waving at?" Aimee asked as they hurried along.

"No one," Madison said, still looking over at Ivy. "No one at all."

After dinner that night, Madison logged online. She owed Bigwheels a big e-mail—and she had plenty to report.

From: MadFinn
To: Bigwheels
Subject: Re: The Whole Story
Date: Tues 3 April 7:30 PM
Thanks for what you wrote. I am glad to know ur friendship with Lainie is still cool. Like I said, ur situation was NOTHING like me and my enemy number one, Ivy. You and Lainie are BFFs and that means something.

I want you to open the picture on this e-mail that I am attaching just for you. Did you know that the butterfly is a symbol of life and friendship? (I read that somewhere.) Of course you probably know that already because you are sooo smart. You can pass it on to Lainie if you want. Maybe she'll like it 2.

Hope you are feeling MUCH better.

Yours till the spring rolls,

Madison

P.S. That's my real name, BTW, not
Madeline. And ur name is so pretty—
I meant to tell you that. I've
never known anyone named Victoria.

<<attachment>>: butterfly.jpg

While she was online, Madison's computer screen
pinged and an Insta-Message appeared from Egg.
Madison feared the worst.

Would Egg launch a counterattack to avenge
what had happened to his friends earlier in the day?
It seemed like something he might do—just to be
extra annoying.

```
<TheEggMan>: Maddie you rock!
<MadFinn>: huh
<TheEggMan>: YOU ROCK!!! I heard
    what happened in science class
    LOL
<MadFinn>: it wasn't nice of us, I
    know
<TheEggMan>: what r u talkin about?
    IT WAS AWESOME
```

```
<MadFinn>: maybe I'm a traitor
<TheEggMan>: what
<MadFinn>: like u said on the bus
   on the field trip—a traitor
<TheEggMan>: what r u saying? it
   was COOL what u did
<MadFinn>: now I'm confused
<TheEggMan>: TMA those losers
   deserved it
<MadFinn>: but they're ur friends
<TheEggMan>: so what they deserved
   it wicked funny stuff I am still
   laffing
<MadFinn>: it was kind of funny
   when they presented to the
   teacher
<TheEggMan>: YES totally!
<MadFinn>: is this y u messaged me?
<TheEggMan>: yeah well and to ask
   how's Fiona?
<MadFinn>: she's fine why don't u
   just call her yourself and see
<TheEggMan>: yeah look I gotta run
<MadFinn>: fine
<TheEggMan>: W-E
<TheEggMan>: *poof*
```

Madison smiled to herself. Egg tried to be so tough sometimes, as if he didn't care about Fiona or about being Madison's best guy friend. But in the end he did care about *all* of it. He was her friend in spite of his constant teasing, taunting, and overall snickering.

And she was his friend, too—even if he was a boy.

Madison opened up a new file.

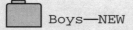 Boys—NEW

> **Rude Awakening:** How come stupid stuff feels so smart when you're in the middle of doing it?
>
> The worst thing about science class today is that I feel like I dissed Hart. Even though Egg said it was funny, I have to think of a way to make it up to Hart. I STILL HAVE THE HUGEST CRUSH ON HIM! I am so sure that now that the science project is over, Ivy will be back to her old tricks. She'll be after him again, too, I bet.
>
> Starting tomorrow, I will be nice to him—and all boys.

As Madison was saving her document, she heard voices downstairs and the sound of a door shutting. Someone was in the living room with Mom, and he had a deeper-than-deep voice.

Madison rushed over to the den to see who was there.

"Madison!" Mom cried when she saw her daughter appear in the doorway. "You remember Paul, don't you?"

Madison nodded. "Sorta."

Paul extended his hand to shake Madison's. She shook back but let go real fast.

"Well," Paul said. "Your mom has been telling me so much about you. She says you've been super-busy."

Madison nodded again. "Uh-huh."

"What are you working on today?" Paul asked.

"Nothing," Madison said, still restricting her responses to two syllables.

Mom didn't like the way Madison was behaving, but she didn't say anything embarrassing. Actually, she didn't say much of anything. She was just smiling.

It was the same look Madison noticed after Mom's first date with Paul.

Rat-a-tat-tat.

There was a knock on the glass sliding doors in the kitchen, and Billy the contractor appeared—gap-toothed grin and all. He'd been out in the backyard, repairing shingles on the side of the house. Mom decided to hire him for a few smaller jobs after he finished fixing the leaky chimney and roof.

"Well, hello," Billy said to Madison when he came into the kitchen. He was looking for a glass of water.

Madison shrugged. "Hi," she said.

Ring, ring.

No sooner had Billy appeared than the telephone

rang. Mom was still busy talking to Paul, so Madison answered it.

"Hey, Dad," she said into the receiver. He was talking quickly from inside his car.

"On my way—over—no Stephanie—dinner—want to go—bowling again?" Dad asked. His voice kept getting cut off from the cell-phone static.

"Sure," Madison said. "See you in a little while."

"Who was that?" Mom asked after Madison hung up the phone.

"Dad's on his way," Madison replied.

"It's early," Mom said. "Gee, that's a switch. Your father is early! I like that." She smiled.

Madison smiled back.

As she glanced around the room, Madison saw Paul shuffling through papers at the kitchen table. Next to the kitchen sink, Billy poured himself a second glass of water. Meanwhile Dad was somewhere in Far Hills racing through traffic to get to the house.

Like swarms of bees, the guys in Madison's and her mom's life were buzzing around tonight. But the date, the fix-it guy, the big D—none of it stung the way it had last week. Things were different now, although Madison wasn't exactly sure why or how they'd gotten that way.

The only thing she knew for sure was that she'd be saving this date in her memory banks for a long time to come.

Today, for the first time, Madison didn't feel

scared about Dad liking Stephanie or Mom dating—even if that meant her dating Paul.

Today, for the first time, Madison didn't feel worried about being on the same side as Ivy—even if it meant being a superstar in class. She knew who her *real* friends were, and they mattered way more than a stupid science contest.

And today, for the very first time, Madison just didn't feel like checking in with some online calendar—or any kind of schedule. She'd let herself be surprised about the next thing that might happen.

And maybe—just maybe—the surprise would involve a certain someone whose named started with *H.*

Mad Chat Words:

=8-o	Shocked
%-6	Brain-dead
{ (i)}	Butterfly
YR	Yeah, right
TAW	Teachers are watching
GGN	Gotta go now
TLGO	The list goes on
And O and O	And on and on
N2M	Not too much
e-z	Easy
GIWIST	Gee, I wish I said that
TMA	Take my advice

Madison's Computer Tip

It's easy to be a poser online, isn't it? When Chet tried to fool me with his note about science class, I almost fell for it, especially since his screen name is so close to his sister Fiona's screen name. I fooled him right back this time—but what if I hadn't? Who knows what other pranks people could pull in a chat room or in an e-mailbox? **Be careful about what you read and respond to online.** Check your e-mail sources carefully if you ever have questions about something that's written to you. Don't let yourself be fooled!

Visit Madison at www.madisonfinn.com

Take a sneak peek at the new

From the Files of

Madison Finn

#8: Picture-Perfect

Chapter 1

Madison dropped onto Fiona's bed and bounced lightly. "Let's hear some tunes," she said, pointing to the digital clock radio on Fiona's nightstand.

Aimee clicked it ON and surfed for a station they liked. A high-pitched voice sang a familiar melody.

And I know (boom, boom)
Yes, I do
From the moment we met
Yes, us two

"Oh my God!" Aimee squealed. "It's NIKKI!"

"Turn it up," Madison yelled.

The two girls bounced on and off the edge of Fiona's bed, singing every lyric along with the radio.

1

I wanna be closer still
There's a place in my heart that you fill
I could be what you want
I know this is true

Aimee leaped up and twirled around, striking a pose like she was singing into a microphone.

Madison fell backward onto the bed laughing.

"What are you guys doing?" Fiona asked, walking back into the room with a tray of juice boxes and chocolate-chip cookies.

"Nikki's on the radio!" Aimee said, still dancing.

I could be sugar sweet like you
Sugar, sugar sweet

Fiona smiled. She put the tray down on her nightstand and the three friends joined together in a circle.

"SUGAR SWEET!" they squealed as the last chorus ended and Nikki's voice faded away.

"This is Stevie Steves and you're listening to WKBM KABOOM! Far Hills radio," the announcer's voice roared across the airwaves once the song finished. "And that was sugar sweet superstar Nikki performing her number-one smash hit 'Sugar Sweet Like You.'"

"I LOVE that song!" Madison said.

2

The announcer continued. "But that's not all, listeners. Get this! Nikki is coming to Far Hills. Stay tuned for details. . . ."

Madison, Aimee, and Fiona stopped short, jaws open.

"Did he just say—?" Madison gasped.

"Oh my God!" Aimee said.

Fiona sat down on the edge of her bed near the radio. "Shh! Shh! Let's listen and hear what they have to say!"

As the radio commercial finished, Stevie Steves came back onto the radio. "Tune in to win tickets to Nikki right here!"

"SHE'S COMING TO FAR HILLS?" Aimee screeched. "WE CAN WIN?"

"Shh!" Fiona hushed. "My mom will hear us."

Aimee couldn't contain her excitement. She continued to jump around the room.

Knock, knock.

The three friends looked at each other, sure that Mrs. Waters had heard. Fiona went to open the door, but Chet poked his head inside before she could get there.

"Keep it down in there," Chet barked. "Quit screaming."

"Get out of my room, dork!" Fiona snapped back, throwing a shoe at the door.

"You're the dork!" Chet shot back, slamming the door behind him.

Madison and Aimee just laughed.

"I'm glad I don't have a brother," Madison said, grabbing a cookie.

Aimee put her hands on her hips. "Yeah, and I have *three*. Lucky me."

Fiona stuffed a cookie in her mouth too, but Aimee said she didn't want one. "How can you guys eat at a time like this? We have a chance to win tickets to a Nikki concert!"

Madison took another bite. "Mmmmmmm?"

"What does that have to do with anything, Aim?" Fiona said.

The radio announcer came back on with all the contest details. "To win, all you need to do is to call us here at WKBM KABOOM! And if you're the lucky random caller, you may be chosen as a super Nikki ticket winner. That means *four* tickets for you and your closet friends."

"We could *all* go!" Madison said. "This is so exciting!"

"Okay, I'm going to call," Fiona said, turning down the volume on the radio and picking up the phone receiver.

Fiona had her very own phone right there in her bedroom. It was the coolest shade of grape-purple, and Madison loved the rainbow stickers Fiona had used to decorate the handle.

"Call NOW!" Stevie Steves said.

Fiona dialed the number for *WKBM*.

"Oh, it's busy," Fiona growled, hanging up and then dialing again. Luckily, she had a redial button on her phone.

But it was still busy *twenty* tries later.

"Keep trying," Aimee insisted. "Keep trying."

Knock, knock.

Chet poked his head in the door.

"What do you want?" Fiona yelled.

"Are you on the phone or what? I want to use it," Chet said. "You can't hog it all the time."

Fiona put her hands on her hips. "You have to wait. I'm using it right now."

Madison and Aimee giggled.

"What are you dorks laughing about?" Chet asked, glaring at them.

"GET OUT OF MY ROOM, CHET!" Fiona screeched again.

"If you're not off the phone soon, I'm telling Mom," Chet threatened.

Fiona snarled. "Fine," as Chet walked out in a huff, slamming the door behind him.

Without missing a beat, Fiona picked up the phone and dialed the radio station once again. *Still busy.* She tried for at least five minutes as Madison and Aimee watched. After hitting redial about a hundred times more, Fiona's eyes grew wide.

"It's RINGING!" she squealed, pressing her ear to the receiver. "It's RINGING!"

Madison and Aimee leaned in close to see what would happen.

"Did they answer?" Aimee asked.

"Shhh!" Fiona said. Her eyes got even wider. "Hello?"

Madison could hear soft voices on the radio in the background, so she went over to listen. Stevie Steves was about to talk to his tenth random ticket winner of the day.

Aimee covered her mouth with her palms so she wouldn't scream.

"Hello?" Fiona said again. "Yes, I was calling to win Nikki tickets."

She looked like she was about to faint.

"What are they saying? What are they saying?" Aimee asked. She started bouncing on the bed again.

"I WON?" Fiona screeched. "Oh, sorry about that," she apologized to the person on the other end of the phone. "I didn't mean to scream but did I really and truly win tickets to the concert?"

Fiona listened closely, cheeks flushed. She gave the phone operator her name and then they put her on hold.

"They want me to wait," Fiona blurted to Madison and Aimee. "They said I'm gonna be on the radio in a few minutes. With Stevie Steves!"

The three friends let out an enormous squeal. Fiona almost dropped the phone.

Madison couldn't turn up the radio to hear because of feedback, so she and Aimee leaned in close while Fiona talked on the phone on the other side of the bedroom.

"This is Stevie Steves back again with the winner of the hour," the announcer said. "We have Fiona on the line. Fiona, are you there?"

Fiona froze. She said nothing.

"Fiona, are you *there*?" Stevie Steves asked again.

Madison and Aimee shot a look in Fiona's direction, which snapped Fiona out of her overexcited trance.

"I'm HERE," she blurted. "Did I win?"

"You sure did," Stevie Steves said. "So tell me, are you a Nikki fan?"

Before Fiona could even answer, Aimee let out another squeal. Madison did too. Fiona joined in. The announcer heard it *all*.

"So, you're a fan—and you're there with friends?" the announcer asked, chuckling to himself. "Either that or we've got some very large mice in the background there."

"We're all the hugest fans of Nikki in the whole world," Fiona gushed. "The HUGEST. Absolutely."

"Well, you and three friends have won tickets to Nikki's exclusive Far Hills concert in two weeks. Stay on the line and our operator will get all your information," he explained. "And listeners, you should stay tuned to WKBM for more great music in the coming hour."

Fiona gave the switchboard at the station her information and hung up the phone. They would have to call back and confirm the win with a parent since Fiona was under sixteen.

"This is so awesome," Aimee said. "I'm shaking."

"Nobody ever wins tickets," Madison said, hugging Fiona tightly around the waist. "I can't believe you won!"

"We all won," Fiona said, grinning from ear to ear. "And now we're going to our very first concert *together*."